Praise for *How You See Me*

We hope you enjoy this book. Please return or renew it by the due date.

You can renew it at www.norfolk.gov.uk/libraries or by using our free library app.

Otherwise you can phone 0344 800 8020 - please have your library card and PIN ready.

You can sign up for email reminders too.

HOW YOU SEE ME

HOW
YOU
SEE
ME

S.E. CRAYTHORNE

First published in 2015 by

Myriad Editions
59 Lansdowne Place
Brighton BN3 1FL

www.myriadeditions.com

1 3 5 7 9 10 8 6 4 2

A CIP catalogue record for this book
is available from the British Library

ISBN (pbk): 978-1-908434-56-2
ISBN (ebk): 978-1-908434-57-9

Designed and typeset in Palatino
by Linda McQueen, London

Printed by CPI Group (UK) Ltd
Croydon CR0 4YY

For Mum, Heidi and John

'Everyone is the hero of their own story.'

Hayley Webster, *Jar Baby*

10th September 2005
Manchester

Dear Mab –

I tried to phone the hospital, but the ward sister couldn't track you down. This should arrive just before me. I'm on my way, so don't – either of you – go anywhere. If Dad gets moved or anything just leave word at the desk – or whatever they have – and I'll find you. Do the same if he gets any better and decides not to see me.

I phoned the 'charlatan' (I told Aubrey you call him that, by the way). He's given me time off work to visit Dad. He said that, on consulting his notes, I appeared to have all the tools I needed to watch my father die. Perhaps we could replace 'charlatan' with 'arsehole'? I held my temper by imagining your response. Still, I'm coming.

I'm probably pulling into the car park now. Find a window and wave.

Daniel

From the pillow next to yours

Dear Alice –

You are sleeping while I write this.

You were sleeping when I opened the letter from my sister. I picked up the post from my flat on my way here

1

tonight. My father is very ill and I have to leave right away. You'll say I should have woken you, but there's too much to say. Too much I haven't said. A father and a sister. A whole life to explain. I'm sorry I've not told you about any of this before; we've had so little time together. I've probably lied to you. That's habit. I lie to everyone about my family.

You are the only person I have ever seen sleep fiercely. Aren't we meant to look our most innocent when we sleep? Like little children. You look as though you're defending something. Your hands are curled into fists and you're frowning, as if you're ready to fight. But your lips are soft.

You were sleeping when I kissed you goodbye.

I'm not sure how long I'll be gone. I'll write when I know what's happening. I wish I could stay. I wish I could gather you up and take you with me. My sleeping warrior. You'd make an excellent talisman. I think I might need one.

Missing you already, my darling,

Your Daniel

12th September
Dad's hospital bed

Dear Mab –

What you didn't have to do was run out on me! I only saw you for two minutes, and you disappeared. I am here. I turned up, just like I said I would. I didn't want to be here, but I was ready to do – I was already *doing* – anything you wanted me to do. And you vanish!

To tell you the truth – and what point is there in telling you anything else? – I'm so angry I can barely write. And I'm *writing*, for Christ's sake! With a *pen*! No number! Not even an email address! Who leaves a PO Box address for their own brother?

I hope this scrawl reaches you. If I could find the tools, I would have cut the words into the page. But, instead, I borrowed a pen from the nurse and was told not to damage it. Observant, these nurses – I must look murderous. Get back here, before they have me arrested!

I'm not the person to do this, Mab. Please don't make me.

Daniel

PS Eleven down was *jug*.

13th September
Hospital

Dear Alice –

Yesterday, I met my sister for the first time in nine years. Actually I met her feet. They were crossed, propped up on my father's hospital bed. She was wearing a pair of those knitted slipper socks they ship over from Tibet or somewhere like that, leather soles clumsily stitched to the feet. I could see the imprint of each toe on those dirty leather soles and a well-trodden sticky patch of what looked like gum. She looked up from her crossword and smirked.

'You look as if you're waiting to be announced.'

Her daughter, Freya, wasn't with her and Mab avoided my questions about her. I would have sat in the chair next to her but she moved her feet over from the bed and started up some yogic stretching. I sat on the edge of Dad's bed to watch her. I had to shift his legs; they felt like nothing more than fallen branches.

Mab's looking old. She's only thirty-four, yet there are wrinkles and grey hairs and even glasses on a ribbon round her neck. She caught me staring. 'Watching my wickedness catch up with me?' She gathered up a pile of jumpers and scarves from her chair – more woollens. 'I can't make anything of eleven down; do what you can. I need coffee.'

She brushed my hair and Dad's arm with the same gesture and left. That was last night; I'm still waiting for her to come back.

I wish I were writing you love letters, instead of all this garbage about my family. I wish I could call you, but I think if I heard your voice I'd run home right now. Are you seeing Aubrey? I know your session is booked for today. It's usually the highlight of my week. I hate to think of you sitting in that office. I hate to think any of it can exist without me there to witness it.

Your Daniel xx

PS And she lied about the crossword. Even Mab could have got the Keats reference.

15th September
The Private Suite

Dear Mab –

Thank you for the cheque and for the letter. And for calming me down – you always were the only one who could do that. I do understand. But this has to be temporary. I have a life now and I like it. I can't be here when Dad gets back to himself. We both know what he thinks of me then.

He's much the same for now, but they've moved us into a side room. We have four walls of our very own! I don't know if this is due to Dad's snoring, or the nurses trying to hide the fact that I'm squatting in the hospital.

They were very sweet about ignoring the visiting hours at first, but when it became clear that Dad wasn't going anywhere they started dropping hints about me leaving. I had the 'freshen up' and the 'go and get some proper sleep' lines dropped on me, quickly followed by my presence being described as 'inappropriate' and 'against regulations'. But I have withstood them all and here I sit. They think I am either monumentally stupid or monumentally devoted. Or perhaps they're planning to barricade the doors the next time I visit the cafeteria? But I just can't face driving to the village or going back into the studio. It makes me feel sick. Probably best I stay here – at least there are plenty of doctors. Aubrey would approve.

Dad's out of it most of the time, but I'll be sitting next to his bed doing the crossword or reading a book and glance over to find him staring at me. I don't think he knows me. He doesn't look angry or horrified, just blank. There's still no speech, but the doctor says that's normal and to give him time. I wish they'd let me put his glasses on. I can't remember if he used to sleep in them or not. He doesn't seem right without his glasses on and a cigarette in the corner of his mouth. It's like something's been amputated from his face.

The nurse just now smiled at me as she came and went. They must have just given up on moving me. She asked me how far I'd come and, when I mentioned Manchester, said I'd brought the weather with me. The window was dark and catching splashes from the first of the rain. You don't notice it in here. It's like its own little world: sanitised, over-lit and overheated. I hope I managed a laugh at the nurse's little joke. I need to stay on their good side. It is rather a horrible image, though, isn't it? Me driving down here, towing a dark cloud behind me like some sinister kite.

Daniel

17th September
The Studio

Dear Alice –

I thought I hated this house, but being back in it is more confusing than hateful. There was no clichéd shiver down my spine or harp-accompanied wash of memories as I stepped over the threshold. Pathetically, I think that's what I'd expected.

It's a house; just a house. A long-abandoned stage set for my childhood memories. I just have to learn to tread the boards again.

That's not to say there's no familiarity. Everything is in its place. Let me give you the tour. From the front door you walk into the living room, with the wood-burner like a living eye in the wall. Beyond that are the kitchen and the bathroom, both with their naked concrete floors and windows overlooking the ragged garden. Upstairs, there is the studio, with the small cupboard bedroom to the side, which Dad used to sleep in before he moved downstairs. And tucked away in the attic is my childhood room and Mab's. A simple house, that's all it is. Yet running up the stairs, the smell of oils and turpentine, catching the wall as I turn into the kitchen, even fumbling for the lock on the bathroom door, is like a haunting. Only, I'm haunting myself.

Obviously last time I was here I was smaller, but I've always been awkward. I was too large for this house at fifteen. My feet were too loud on its floors; my shoulders banged against doorframes, my head against the beams. I was like your namesake after too much cake. All those long-healed bruises are ripening again.

One of my father's models, Kirsty, was a dancer. She used to talk about muscle memory, working the dance into your bones. Like the characters of Mab's masks that seem to stick to even the most sceptical actors. Have you ever seen mask work? It terrifies me.

I don't want to be the person I left behind in this house. I don't want to remember. I want to be with you, wrapped in your hair, your legs and your sheets. I want to fall asleep on your breasts, with my hands full of your flesh, my head full of your scent.

But whatever I want, like it or not, I'm home.

Your Daniel xx

19th September
The Studio

Dear Mab –

The first difficulty was getting Dad out of the car. It takes an age to rouse him to any action and I still haven't learnt how to deal with him. I keep thinking of the nurses in the hospital:

'Just pop your head up there, Michael.'

'That's the way, right foot; now the left. Nearly there, Michael, you're doing nicely.'

Apparently the key is a soft and determined tone, as though you're whispering to a fractious horse, and to use his name repeatedly, as if you're in a bad radio play. Patronise, never be afraid to patronise. But that's what I'm afraid of – ending up like Aubrey! I never thought I'd say it, but Dad's been through enough without having his hulk of a son frisking him for his keys on the doorstep while muttering on and on about how 'nearly there' we are.

We were met by your letter, which was most welcome and gave me something to read in a normal voice after I'd got him into his chair.

I'd been back to the house briefly to check on things, but someone (I suspect Maggie – I could smell her in the Jeyes Fluid) had been in and done between times. There are cyclamen everywhere. I hate cyclamen. Half of them look near death and are just stubby corms cresting though the soil. Those flowers are too delicate; I always think I'm going to crush them. And the little tables she'd put them on – dragged from God knows where – have given me something else to walk into. Still, she's sorted out milk and bread and everything else I'd forgotten. But it's too clean in here; it looks shorn and pressed and not quite itself. Like poor Dad.

(Later)

I'd forgotten this house has a will of its own. I fired up the wood-burner, even though it's so mild – Dad's got used to hospital temperatures and kept shivering no matter how many pieces of clothing I pulled on to him. We were sitting peacefully drinking our umpteenth cup of tea – another hospital habit – and I started itching. The rug in the living room is alive with fleas! They're everywhere. I'll have to go into town and get something to blitz them.

Dad was restless until I switched on the TV. He seems to like the sound and the colours flashing over the screen. He still hasn't got his glasses; they're somewhere in the bags. I tried putting them on him before we left the hospital, but they looked too big for him – or his face looked too small, I don't know.

I went outside and sat on the doorstep with a cigarette, picking black fleas off my ankles and cracking them between my thumbnails; examining my own blood. There is a row of roses that has been dug in along the side of the house, rattling with dead leaves. I jumped at a skittering around their roots (you know how I feel about rats – Winston Smith has nothing on me!) only to see a couple of brown birds appear. Tame, but interested. Perhaps someone's been feeding them? Surely not Dad?

And, at the risk of confirming myself as the Great, Huge Bear returned home, someone's been sleeping in my bed! I don't mean it's been made up; someone has just got out of it. The sheets pulled back and twisted and the shape of a woman curled and then removed. It smells of perfume. Her books are splayed and piled on the carpet, including a couple of Dad's old sketchbooks, the gluey pats of oil paint stuck in the pile. I keep wondering who she is. My own personal Goldilocks!

Daniel

22nd September
Missing you!

Dear Alice –

You're a pleasure to write to and somehow that pleasure is more real when I write than if I tried to call you. I imagine myself talking to you, and I can see just how you would listen: that hand scanning your face for blemishes which never exist, teasing out your hair, tugging and readjusting your clothes; your eyes anywhere but on my face. You worry about your appearance of restlessness, of a lack of interest, but it's one of the things I love best about you. You are the one person who listens and understands. At least you try to understand.

Maggie came today. Maggie was an immense part of my childhood. Literally. Maggie was a tanker, a fatty, a blimp; she had two truck legs and a blubber butt; if Maggie jumped in, the water would jump out. This I learnt when I made the mistake of inviting a friend to tea. The next day at school was full of taunts. Charlie Gibson had told everyone about 'that big fat woman with no knickers that cooked us eggs'.

Until Mab put a stop to it. Maggie's father was a butcher. His favourite boast was that he could feed three families with one slice off his daughter's hind.

Maggie was, for a time, my father's favourite model. She was certainly the one we loved best. Sturdy and oversized child that I was, it was my great ambition to be able to hug Maggie all the way round. Until then I had to love her portion by portion, hanging off whatever giant limb or bulge came my way. She mothered me, I suppose. Poor motherless mite. She fed me and loved me and did her best.

She caught me at an awkward moment today. Dad was down for his mid-morning nap and I was missing you. There's no internet here so – oh, I hope you'll understand this! – I went to Dad's studio and sorted through canvases searching for artistic pornography. You know my dad's style. It's always the model looking down at herself. I was looking for a body I could mistake for you. There was a girl I remembered, but I couldn't find the sketch. It's probably hanging in a gallery somewhere.

Maggie never knocks; she walks in. I don't think she guessed what I was up to. Models forget that nudes have anything to do with sex, and, as I said, Maggie is one of the best. She's shrunk. All those beautiful swells of flesh have ebbed away. She's an old balloon. An old lady.

'You're up here, then, with the girls. Should have known it.'

I left the paintings and moved over to kiss her and throw an arm over her shoulders. Even standing straight I could have fitted her under my chin. We've become perfect dancing partners. It wasn't long before she shook me off.

11

'Enough of that.' I don't know when we stopped touching each other, but it was years before I left. They're odd here, with their rules for children, their rules for young men.

She squinted up at me. 'Your dad's sleeping. I got him a blanket from the box. Better get ourselves back downstairs and give him some company. You can show me whether you can make a decent cup of tea after all these years.'

I was glad of the smile.

We had a nice visit, all in all. She bossed me about the kitchen and rearranged the cleaning products I bought the other day in town, sniffing at labels that didn't meet her standards. It was only as she was leaving that she came out with it. About 'that business'.

'I never believed your dad when he told me. I mean about that girl. I told him you must have got yourself confused. Well, it happens, doesn't it? And a boy like you, after what your mum did to herself. I know, I know, I'm not going over all that now. But it was bound to affect you, wasn't it? That's why you got confused.

'But you're grown now and back with your dad. It's a good thing you're doing, Danny. And there'll be no more confusion now, will there? No more of that business.'

I want to come home to you, Alice. I've had enough of this. I'll write to Mab; I don't care how much work she's got on. I have a job too, after all. And I have you. I need to get out of here.

Running towards you,
Dxx

24th September
The Studio

Dear Aubrey –

I told you I'd be in contact when I knew more and I was going to phone this week. However, after your letter, I thought it would be better to write.

I appreciate my absence is difficult for you and the last couple of weeks must have been trying, but the fact that I was called away was not my fault. You were generous enough to give me leave and I thought that was because you understood. My father is very ill. I'm afraid there have been a series of strokes. He can't speak or take care of himself. So I have to take care of him. There's no one else to do it. This is hardly a holiday.

All of my notes and final drafts are filed in the computer in the usual way. You can access them using your password. If hard copies are missing then I can only presume they have been misfiled or mislaid. And, if that has happened, it was certainly not my oversight. The implication that I would steal from you is frankly offensive. Why would I have any use for any client's files? I would have hoped, after the years we have spent working together, that I would have earned a certain degree of trust.

Yours,
Daniel Laird

25th September
Still here

Dear Mab –

I've been rewriting this letter for days. It's strange having so much time to think. Too much time. I'm not neglecting Dad, but he's still too ill to be considered company.

The point of this letter – now I'm finally writing it – is that I need to go home. I can't stay here any longer. Dad's getting better every day and you may have forgotten what he thinks of me, but I don't think he has. Not really. The doctors said the brain heals quickly. It's strange thinking of all those neurons linking up in there. Couple more connections and he'll remember he hates me. I'm scared every morning when I wake him that this will be the morning he finally recognises me. Then it will all happen like before.

(Later)

OK, I'll be honest. I have met a girl. She's a patient of Aubrey's – which of course means there's nothing wrong with her (apart from trusting Aubrey, and we've all been guilty of that). Her name is Alice.

I met her first through words on a page. Alice Williams. Case Number: 3478. You know the work I do for Aubrey – I see dozens of case files and transcribe hundreds of notes – but this collection of papers was different. It was as if I could smell her perfume on the pages. It was a love letter addressed to me.

Sure, she has her problems. She cries too easily and quakes with a general fear of life, but it's not incapacitating.

It's nothing Aubrey couldn't sort out with a handful of his magic white pills and a quick daddy chat. Still, he signed her up for the full twelve-week course of one-to-one therapy – something it is obvious she can ill afford. And, Mab, I found I was grateful. As soon as I read her words, I wanted to read more. There is a tenderness, a sweetness in her speech that even Aubrey's callous shorthand cannot obscure. Alice was simply luminous on the page.

After I saw her outside Aubrey's office – I waited after her regular twelve o'clock appointment – I realised I'd seen her before, at the Art Gallery a few months ago. She was standing between Nude #62 and Nude #68, looking up at *Hylas and the Nymphs*. You remember how Dad insisted the Waterhouse remain *in situ* during his exhibition? I don't even know why I was there; I usually avoid Dad's shows. But the Laird exhibition had caused such a stir in Manchester and maybe I just wanted a wander down Memory Lane.

It was Alice's hair that made the impression. She's a blonde, and if you met her you'd say she wore it short, but actually it's this mass of tight spirals. God knows how long that hair would be if you brushed it straight. But it was that cloud of yellow I remembered. She thrusts her fingers into it as she speaks. It's like some kind of power source: her speech speeds up after that gesture. It's remarkable hair – electric hair. More impressive than tears or trembling. More a symbol of her true self.

(Later)

It's impossible to write any of this without hearing your reply. Your voice interrupts every sentence. There is no need to remind me of my own mistakes. They are *mine* after all; I'm hardly likely to forget them. Alice is not a mistake. This doesn't mean you needn't reply – just try to make it unpredictable: tell me I can go home.

D.

28th September
A sweet dream

Dear Alice –

I am between your legs, my elbow pressed against the floor of your thigh. Parting the silk of your hair to find the beauty of your cunt. Your body rolls away from me like a landscape. I drink in the scent of you. Your smell is my discovery. It blossoms alongside the perfume of the hyacinths on your bedroom sill. I know when you planted those bulbs: you explained the dirt on your fingers when you came to your session. And now I find them breaking the soil, blooms drawn out by the heat. Between your legs and in your room, discovering you inch by inch.

Your smell is freshly turned earth, a freshly cut vein. I paint it on my fingertips. I want to daub it on my pulses, the way expensive women wear expensive perfume. The taste of you is the change of texture under my tongue, the secret warmth and flavour that makes you moan and twist. I know everything about you and still there is more to explore.

Crawling up your body, over your mounds and through your dells, letting my tongue run behind my gaze. Already nostalgic for where I have travelled, yet eager for what's to come. There are so few adventures in my life. Your face is turned aside, and I'm in your hair. I tease free a strand and lay it in my palm, watching it curl and move. It reminds me of those cellophane fortune fish you get in Christmas crackers, coiling and recoiling in the heat from my hand. You remind me of the first woman I ever loved. A girl with masking tape in her hair and charcoal dust blackening the soles of her feet. But her story is not ours. We will have a happy ending.

You are the diary of my desires and you are too far away. But I am with you, Alice, even if they will not let me leave here.

Yours, always yours,
Daniel xx

1st October
The Studio

Dear Mab –

The tiniest incidents make a day.

This morning Dad sat obediently in the bath and waited for me to wash him. I was surprised. I had to help him in, of course, and help him undress the best I could. He insisted on folding each piece of clothing and laying it carefully across the toilet seat. Socks balled into each shoe, as if he were going swimming.

I lathered a sponge with soap and eased it over his shoulders. He did nothing to help or hinder me, just accepted it. I wasn't too sure what to do about the bandages on his left leg, so I propped his ankle on a shampoo bottle and worked around them, just dampening the edges of the dressing. There are marks of old breaks in his skin: the bloom of bruises where needles have pressed into him, where they have been taped into place. His body is a chart of scars I can't wash away.

I rinsed him off, dipping and squeezing the sponge. I should get a shower head to fix on the taps. Then he stood up suddenly, without assistance, and I grasped his outstretched arms. There was this little old man in a bathtub, his white hair sleek and steaming, a tube linking his prick to the bag of urine resting on the neatly folded clothes. I held his hands and watched the bathwater drip down into the dressing on his leg. The adhesive gave out, and sodden gauze slid into the soapy water.

I bandaged him back up and got him settled in his chair in front of the TV with a cup of tea and a plate of toast. He insists on having the bloody thing at full volume whatever the programme or time of the day. I can't even say he watches it particularly, but he seems content with his eyes on the screen, and it allows me to leave off the mindless chatter I keep up until it's turned on. I think I'm trying to convince him – or should I say remind – that I am an actual person and not some automaton that appears in the morning and disappears at night.

I made myself busy in the kitchen. You would never believe how domestic I've become: I examine every plate and knife and rinse carefully before it leaves the sink; I relish scrubbing the tannin from teaspoons; I polish glasses and hold them to the light. I'm like some underworked barman in the movies. *What can I get you, sir? Scotch straight up and an ear for your troubles?*

I whistle in an attempt to drown out the noise from the TV and follow a routine: fold clean laundry from Maggie; sort rubbish; look over Dad's medication; write tiny shopping lists. It's mindless work, but I like it. Thoughtless hours can fill up a day. There's a peace in it.

By eleven am, I'm on my knees with a plastic bucket getting on with the business of taps and tubes on Dad's ankle. This job goes best if I just get on with it; Dad's usually pretty absorbed in the TV and, if I can empty the catheter bag without disturbing or upsetting him, then I count it a success. Then I can tip the lot down the toilet, wash my hands and go out for a smoke. My reward.

This morning, the bag was emptying, and I was already congratulating myself, when Dad reached out and took hold of my head. It shocked me a bit, but I turned my face up to him and smiled. Think I even said a few words, you know: 'Morning, Dad. Not hurting you, am I?' Something like that. He just sat there and stared at me, right *at* me. He hasn't done that for days, maybe not since we got back here. And, before I could get started with the usual platitudes, he grinned. A proper loving happy smile, holding my head between his hands and looking into my face.

I just knelt there and stared back at him. Eventually some noise or light-flash from the TV caught his attention, his eyes flicked back up to the screen and the smile dimmed, but he kept hold of my head. When my legs started to ache, I twisted round so I was sitting at his feet. He stroked my hair. My head was his pet. I didn't want to leave. We might have sat there like that for an hour or more.

When his hands finally slipped away, I felt cold. I checked the catheter, gathered everything up and got rather

19

awkwardly to my feet. Halfway up, he made a grab for me again, this time squashing my face between his palms. He frowned at me, tilting his head, that way he does at a cigarette that has gone out on him. Then he shoved me over towards the arm rest. The bucket of piss nearly fell out of my hands. I laughed. My head was a cabbage. And it was blocking the TV.

Rewarded myself with two smokes and a bacon sandwich.

> *Everyone's servant,*
> *Daniel*

10th October
The Studio

Dear Mab –

Did you know there was a dog?

Maggie turned up with it yesterday and left without it. She seemed shocked that I didn't remember.

'It's Tatiana, Danny. Princess fucking Tatiana – how could you forget a name like that?'

'We never had a dog,' I replied, folding the animal's ears between my fingers. She seemed friendly enough, but that didn't mean I wanted her in the house.

'Of course you didn't.' Maggie sighed. 'It was that girl's dog, remember? She brought it back with her, anyways. Third-hand by that time, though, I shouldn't wonder. Your dad's had her since.'

'What girl?'

'We call her Tatty,' she finished, proudly, ignoring my question and pointing at the dog.

Cue long calculations of Tatty's age in both human and dog years. This whole conversation was conducted, of course, in the middle of the street. Finally it came to an end when the dog took up barking and we realised Dad was trying to make it down the steps in his long johns.

So now we have a dog (I can't quite bring myself to call her a bitch) and no one seems able to agree on breed. She really does look like a bundle of tatty rags: white, copper and black. I'm sure Freya would love her. She is nice enough and worships Dad. When I got them both inside they settled down to sleep, Tatty like a rug at Dad's feet in front of the wood burner. That at least explains the fleas. I'll have to sort out some powder and some special food. Dog or human years, I suspect I've acquired another ancient.

We're quite the little family, I can't help thinking, sitting here writing to you and watching them sleep. I've even stopped whining for home, I hope you've noticed. Alice is on my mind, but I won't bother you with any more details because, if your last letter was anything to go by, you will never understand. I'll just send you these dull updates of our dull days and you'll keep sending your cheques and your postcards and we'll all get along just fine. Won't we, Mab?

Daniel

21st October
The Studio

Dear Alice –

My sister is inexplicable. She just refuses to let me leave. I'm so sorry, my darling. She's busy, of course, with her masks and her daughter. And Corsica is far enough away for her to ignore my pleas to be back with you. Mab has never understood love; it's not in her character. Queen Mab. No love in her name, either.

We were born into our names, you know. They were already waiting for us. No anxious 'Is it a boy or a girl?' for our parents. My Dad just asked, 'Is it Mabel or Daniel?' and then, 'Is it Agatha or Daniel?' The change in mothers didn't affect that particular question.

We have different mothers, you see. Dad dropped the moneyed and impeccable Eleanor as soon as he glimpsed my pale, frail mother. He left his first wife with his name – Ms Laird, she is to this day – and his daughter, whom she immediately packed off to boarding school for part of the year and back to him for the summer.

Agatha never appeared – the very possibility of her disappeared off the edge of that bridge with my mother when I was four years old – but Mabel and I took our places and our allocated titles.

Mabel Anne Laird. What did they expect when they put that together? Someone steady and reliable, even a little dowdy? Certainly not the raw, screaming, red-fisted infant who fought her way out of the womb to gnaw on her mother's nipples with her sharp pink gums. Vampire baby – suckling blood. Her mother loves to expand on that particular story. Mabel bit her name in two as soon as she could say it. Keeping the first syllable, the one that filled up your mouth, re-shaping it into a grab, a stab. She spat away the softening -*el*.

Mab with a trick up every sleeve; Mab with an answer for everything; Mab, my sister, who saw and heard all there was to see and hear and only spoke the truth when she wasn't lying.

Mab was named for a friend of my father's, a friend I never met but whose Christmas cards would sometimes hang up among the others, strung from beams in the studio. They were unimaginative cards that Mabel sent, obviously selected from a variety pack: plump robins and snowy scenes printed on cheap, flimsy paper. Always the same message: *Hope you're all keeping well! Much love, Mabel xx*. Mab would study these cards intently; I caught her fishing them down from their rope to look again at the message, hunting for clues to the shape our father had wanted her to take.

Mab was her own creation.

As I say, she came to us for the school holidays every year. Strange, that. I remember her as always there, as if life started and ended when Mab came to stay, but actually our close contact spanned a bare handful of summers. After it became clear that I would grow to bear no resemblance to my mother, my dad rather lost interest in me. The models brought me up, but it was nice to have real family to hand.

When she was fifteen, frankly too old to be hanging around with us, Mab turned up sporting the lipstick, the rolled-up skirt and the chewing-gum-smacking insolence that had signified her move into secondary school. My friends and I were playing on Marchmount Street, between the studio and the church. The tarmac on the road had melted and coated the soles of our sandals so we could pick up gravel from the raised footpath. Hobnail boots. Mab was with us, but apart, picking at her cuticles and leaning up against the church wall. She may even have been sent out to keep an eye on me.

Sebastian Collie walked his bike down the pavement on the other side of the street. Coloured beads ticked along the spokes as the wheels turned. The problem with the Collies was that they'd moved up to the village later than the rest of us. They were the first of the commuters to come, taking advantage of the easy access to the dual carriageway and the otherwise 'idyllic rural surroundings'. They'd settled in one of the new builds that had appeared at the end of our street. Maggie had told us Mrs Collie asked for lime in her gin and tonic when they'd visited the Bull and she wore make-up all day, even first thing in the morning.

Back there on the street, it was Rachel Spencer from my class who was the first to speak to him.

'You're Sebastian from London.'

'Nice hair,' shouted Martin Phillips.

This was true: Sebastian did have nice hair. Not hair like any of ours, but long tresses of blond curls that reached past his shoulders. Hair a bit like yours, my darling, though not as fiery. *It's a shame he's a boy*, I remember Maggie saying to us, *with hair like that*.

We'd seen Sebastian before, in the shop by the bridge. He was standing in the doorway hand in hand with his little sister whose name I never knew. Both were dressed in neatly ironed London clothes. They were staring at Jack's tractor which was parked out front. I had wanted to grab those beautiful locks and stuff a handful into my pocket. I imagined it would feel like the spun sugar Maggie had boiled up for us in the studio kitchen. Long strands of gold: brittle, slippery and sticky, all at the same time. I could break off a piece and pop it in my mouth, feel it dissolve.

'Only girls have hair like yours,' Mab called from her place by the church wall. 'Are you a girl, Sebastian?'

I can't remember him speaking. Try as I might, I can't remember the sound of Sebastian Collie's voice. He may have shaken his head, or maybe he just tried to walk on and leave us behind. I think that's what I would have done. Maybe he just stood there.

The others took up the call, and I suppose my voice joined them. 'Girl! He's a girl! Sebastian Collie wears dresses! He wears skirts! Want a go with my skipping rope, Sebastian?' We surrounded him; we caged him in, still gripping the handlebars of his new bike. There was no escape.

I don't know when the shoving started; I don't know when Mab joined us, but I know it was her voice that shouted, 'If he's a boy, he better prove it. Let's pull down his pants and see.'

We took hold of him, pressing him down on to the sticky tarmac. He was small, and we were stronger than him. His arm was pale and rounded like a doll's, his skin rubbery as he twisted under my hands. I don't remember him saying a word.

I don't know what it was that made us pull back. I'd like to think it was a moment of self-awareness: that we suddenly saw ourselves and what we were doing. Maybe it was Sebastian's silence, his lack of any real resistance. Someone probably thought they saw a grown-up coming. Mab must have gone home, because it was just me and my friends. We crossed the street and stood together by the church wall, leaving Sebastian sitting in the road with his bicycle by his side. In the end Martin went over to check on him.

'Pissed himself,' Martin told us when he came back. 'Right through his trousers. It stinks over there.'

The Collie children didn't join us at the local primary school for the next term. Maggie told us their parents had dipped into their university fund to pay for a private school. *Airs and graces*, Maggie said. Sebastian's curls were cut and he had to wear a blazer and a tie. The daily commute to London must have proved too much for Mr Collie, because the family started using the village house only at weekends. Then they put it up for sale. I didn't see much of Sebastian after that. He never rode his bike past the studio; he would take the long route across the fields.

I've often wondered why Mab took against Sebastian like that. Whether, if it weren't for her, anything would actually have taken place. I don't think it was his hair and clothes that offended her so much as his obvious difference from the rest of us. Sebastian had the magazine version of a happy family: Father, Mother, Son and Daughter all lined up in little steps; and, latched to his well-groomed back, he had London. Sebastian Collie had somewhere to escape to.

It was only a year before Mab followed the Collies' example and turned out on to the dual carriageway, away from the village, away from her mother and away from us. After that she never stopped running, but she would always send me postcards from everywhere she visited. I would pin them up round the window frame in my bedroom, a circular chart of my sister's flight from city to city, continent to continent. Their messages were generally simple: *I was here – love to you, Mab*. A biro line would stretch around to the front of the card, where arrowheads plunged into foreign cities, with white houses piled one on top of the other like building blocks or clinging limpet-like to the sides of cliffs; they speared tropical beaches and sun-washed seas; and once even a dirty French street with rubbish piled in its gutters and a street sign reading 'Paradis'.

On occasion, Mab would veer close enough to visit and we would have couple of snatched hours. She would arrive bearing gifts of carved wood, silks and stories, like a visiting foreign merchant, the scents of strange places on her skin. I'd make her breakfast as she filled the ashtray and told me of her adventures. She never had much to say to Dad.

Once, she turned up early in the morning, glittering with coloured beads, her skirts heavy with rainwater; her hair was dreadlocked and she had sewn bells and ribbons into the matted lengths which flapped against her cheeks. A carnival sister. Her face was swollen and she looked as if she hadn't slept in days. It was the only time I managed to convince her to stay the night and meet some of my friends at a burger bar in town. She arrived creaking in a leather suit and stinking of motorbike grease, her hair shorn and twisted into tight little spikes across her brow. Each spike's tip had been dipped into bleach or colour. A row of poisoned arrows. She charmed my friends within minutes. They gathered to share her anecdotes; to taste that wild, loose laughter. I hardly recognised her.

Mab was never one to be captured. Not even by me. I pity the people that attached themselves to her. She did have a way of making you feel important. But there was always somewhere else to be, someone else to meet, and the friends and lovers would be left behind. A row of bodies with biro arrows embedded in their chests. *Mab was here.*

Only once did my father ever try to paint her. It was one of the early summers in the studio. Mab had fallen asleep on the armchair in the work-room. I watched my father creep around her, gathering his paints, slotting the easel into place. He stretched a piece of fabric across the top of the chair, its tattered ends whispering against her brow. He lifted one of her hands and laid it against her cheek. Once satisfied with his composition, he took his place behind the easel. I didn't like it – too sentimental.

When he works with his feet on the floor, my father paints like a fencer, straight-backed, his arm extended in front of him, his brush a foil held in his languid grip. He attacks a canvas with smooth slick strokes, leaning for a moment on his back foot and pausing before his riposte. As Mab slept she was gathered into oils and I trundled my toy train around my father's feet. He whispered to himself as he worked, but I couldn't catch what he said.

Finally, Dad stood back from his painting. A streak of burnt sienna painted a deep scar from his left cheekbone to his lip. He looked exhausted.

I pulled myself to my feet to look at the canvas. There was Mab sleeping in her chair, the throw folded over her, its corner reaching down to her like a beneficent hand. But there were flaws: her nose was wrong, and her lips seemed plumper than I had ever seen them. This was back when

I took my father's work literally. I looked for truth, not beauty. It was not quite her face. I thought there was something wrong with his eyes.

Mab woke up; she stretched and kicked her feet out from under her. Then she saw my father. I had never seen her so angry.

'What are you doing?'

'Oh, you're awake – that's a shame, but I think I've done all I need to today. Come and see, darling. You looked so lovely I couldn't resist. Look what your daddy's made of you.'

'What have you done?'

My father turned the easel and Mab screamed. She ripped the drape down from above her head and balled it.

'Now, Mabel – '

Mab ran at the painting and my father caught her hands before she could push a fist into it.

The next day the painting was missing from the workroom. Maggie found it a week later stuffed into the corner of the woodshed. The frame had been broken and the image, or what remained of it, had been obscured by liberal doses of my black poster paint. Someone had tried to set it on fire; the edges of the torn canvas were rotten with stale ashes. My father took the broken portrait from Maggie without a word. No one was punished. But there were no more family portraits.

From that day on Mab seemed never to sleep if there was anyone there to catch her. She was the blur at the edge of photographs, darting out of shot, swinging her head, faster than any camera shutter. I was always there in the background of those family shots. The little brother, his face lit up by the camera flash, his expression caught in every detail, his eyes following his sister's constant departure. *Watch the birdie, Daniel.*

(Later)

I look back over what I've written and wonder why I've told you all this. If I were reading this letter I would believe my sister to be fierce and brutal and proud and glamorous and even a little dangerous. She is all these, but many other things besides. This is a long letter, but there is not enough paper to tell all the stories and memories I have of just this one person. I have tried to do what my father tried before me, to paint a portrait, and it's as misshapen as his. Mab would hate it.

I know why I'm telling you these things. I feel that I know all of you, because of the hours I've spent writing down your words; but perhaps each of those hours was another flawed portrait. What haven't you told me?

Missing you,
Your Daniel xx

3rd November
The streets of Upchurch

Dear Mab –

Tatty and I went for a walk today. This is not counting our daily trudges at dawn and twilight so I can watch her piss and shit on the tracks round the back field. We have other companions on those jaunts, men and women with their own dogs and discreetly held little bags of dog turd. It took me some time to learn the rules. One woman stopped me pointedly to tell me they were considering starting DNA testing of dogs fouling the pathways. Would I care to sign a petition and agree to Tatty being sampled?

We all make a fuss of each other's dogs and look on like proud parents as they sniff each other's arses. Most of the women, though, seem to know me or someone I went to school with. They ignore me or scuttle past in groups, their dogs placed firmly between us, but I can see them aching for gossip. *I'm* aching for gossip, but I've none to give.

Dad is much as he was. The arrival of the district nurse was the reason for our departure. She's small and pretty and hates Tatty and me in equal measure. I know this because she complains about us loudly to Dad in a stage whisper.

'Should get that son of yours to give you a better wash in the evening, shouldn't we, Michael?'

'I'm sure I've told that son of yours a thousand times how to tie a dressing. But does he listen, Michael?'

'There's that dreadful dog of yours, Michael. Bringing all that mess and dirt up to bother you. Needs a brush, that dog. Sure that son of yours could have a go at that, if he took the time.'

All this in a bright and breezy falsetto and all addressed to Dad. She's so sweet to him, while being so rude to me, that I don't dare question her. Who knows what a replacement would be like? So 'that dog' and 'that son' have made a habit of taking a walk when she arrives.

Love to Freya – I enclose a letter from a furry friend.

Daniel x

Dear Freya –

My name is Tatty. It's short for Princess Tatiana, who was a Russian princess, but I'm a dog so you should call me Tatty. I am a small dog with lots of fur. Some people say I'm not a proper dog because I'm small and because I am made up of lots of different types of dog. But I think that is how the best dogs are made. My fur is different colours: brown and white and black and gold. It hangs together in big locks. I think it looks like feathers.

There are two things I would like best in the world: 1. To fly like a bird, and 2. Lots of friends. Your Uncle Dan is my friend. He takes me for walks, and laughs when I bark at the birds with their clever flying, and feeds me tasty bits of food that Grandad can't finish. Would you be my friend too, Freya? Uncle Dan says you're very nice.

One of my favourite things is the nice warm fire and going to sleep on Grandad's feet. Uncle Dan says that I snore and when I dream my paws go running, but I don't go anywhere. He laughs, but I don't mind. He seems to like laughing.

My biggest secret is that when I dream I don't go running. I go flying. Do you know how secrets work? When someone tells you a secret you have to listen very carefully and then curl it up tight in your mind, as if it's a little bit of paper that you crumple up in your hand. When it is very small, so small you can barely see it, then you have to pretend you are a little dog like me and dig a deep hole. Then you drop the secret into the hole and cover it up with earth. When you've cleaned your paws, nobody else will ever know where to find the secret except you.

Now I've told you a secret, will you tell me one of yours? I like digging holes.

Lots of love and woofs,

Tatty

4th November
The Studio

Dear Aubrey –

I have a case study for you. One I think you'll appreciate. It involves a story that's been told before. Certainly I've heard it or overheard it. Maybe it will bore you, you're the one with all the connections, after all. But it's a story that bears retelling – according to the men of Upchurch, at least.

Man walks into a pub. He shouldn't have left his house, but he's just lost an argument with his sick father for a bottle of whisky and now the sick father is drunk and snoring. It's still early and frankly this man is starved of company. He takes the paper he's already read and its half-completed crossword. He nods to the men standing at the bar and takes his pint and his paper to the corner of the snug.

'Back looking after your dad, are you?' The man at the bar doesn't turn until he has asked the question.

Our guy nods his head and folds up his paper; clicks his pen open and pretends to study the next clue. These sweet steps of masculine etiquette. Do both men know the game they're playing? Another man turns at the bar; both settle back on their elbows, drink in hand, unfavoured foot finding the shelf in the wooden panelling. Our man is observed.

'Who's this, then?'

'This is the artist's boy. Been up north, haven't you, Danny?'

'Danny Laird. Went to school with my Sam, you did. What you up to these days?'

'His dad's just out of the hospital. Stroke, wasn't it?'

'I heard something like, but you never know with our resident artist, do you? Lot of rumours. That girl of Laird's.'

'Not in front of the boy.'

'No, you're right there. Still up at Miracle's place?'

'Now there's a name I haven't heard for years.'

'You know that story about Miracle, do you, Danny?'

Of course he knows the story – it helped make him… but he keeps his mouth shut. It's not often you get to hear your life discussed by strangers while you're in the same room.

'Lives in Miracle's house, doesn't he? And it's not like old Maggie is one to hold her tongue when there's something to be said.'

'That's no story you'd tell a kid.'

'Never know what went on in that house. Naked girls doing flits across the garden.'

'You'd know all about that, Ron. Wasn't your wife one of them?'

'She wasn't the one that ran screaming.'

'Not in front of the boy.'

Would they notice if Danny Laird got up and walked away? Is he necessary to this plot?

'Miracle was the name he got from that illness he had as a kid. There was something growing in his brain and no hospital or doctor could do a thing to stop it. Then there was talk about some special operation in America. Said it was his last hope. My dad used to talk about that mother of his walking up and down the streets with a plastic ice-cream tub, photo of the boy stuck to the side of it, begging for donations to help. There was nothing that woman didn't do: sponsored events and letters to all the rich people she could think of. It was worse than the church roof.

'The boy, though – well, he ran wild. Used to plough that bike of his right through the allotments and broke all the windows in one of the sheds. Never saw him at the school. But no one had the heart to chide him, not with him dying and all. The mother had no control and anyway she was too busy with her fund-raising to notice much else that went on.

'Anyhow, they were getting close to their target, but the tumour in his head had its own clock and the doctors here said they'd have to do something soon. America or no America, they were going to operate. Well, the mother was desperate and took up pleading and begging for more time. In the end, probably just to shut the woman up, they agreed to one more scan. And it was gone. That massive tumour had completely disappeared.

'The mother went round and gave everyone back their money, I'll give her that. And Miracle went back to school. That's what they called him in the papers. "The Miracle Boy". Used to have a clipping in a frame up in here at one time.'

'Killed himself, though, didn't he?'

'Blew his brains out.'

'Only in his forties, wasn't he? That's no age.'

'I heard it was his vanity. Some dentist told him he needed a set of false teeth, so he drove home and did himself in.'

'No. He hit that woman on the dual carriageway. Must have been nearly twenty years ago now. Couldn't live with himself after that.'

'Not in front of the boy, Clive.'

'Still, they took his house over, didn't they. Lived there. It's no wonder what happened next.'

Not much of a case study for you really. Certainly not as difficult as today's cryptic proved to be. Pretty easy for you to form a hypothesis and draw a conclusion. But I wonder if it explains anything at all.

> *Regards,*
> *Daniel*

5th November
The Studio

Dear Alice –

A dream last night:

There is a small boy and the boy is me. He is holding his mother's hand. They are walking on a footpath towards a bridge. The bridge is not a real bridge because there is no water to cross. Instead of water there is a road and fast fast cars that never stop, so people have to walk over them instead of through them. There are steps up one side, from house and shops and the footpath, and then steps down the other side to more houses and a school, where the boy is going, and a tall church, where his mother is going.

At the top of the first steps sits a man. A homeless man. He is the first homeless man the boy has ever seen. He is very dirty and he has a blanket under him. The boy stops to look at him. The boy is wearing his school uniform. The trousers are brand new. There are still creases in them where they had been folded into a packet. His mother is wearing a summer dress, though it's not quite summer any more.

The boy calls the homeless man Smiler, because he smiles all the time. The mother gives the boy a fifty-pence piece. Smiler still scares the boy, because he is so strange. The boy sees there is a folded pocket in Smiler's blanket with some coins in it. The folds are there so when you throw your money it will not roll away. The boy lets go of his mother's hand and runs towards Smiler. He drops his coin on to the other coins in Smiler's blanket. Clink. The boy watches to see what will happen, but Smiler just keeps smiling.

Because the boy is watching Smiler, he does not see his mother climb over the railing at the edge of the bridge. He does not see his mother jump into the water that is not water, but road and cars. And he misses the white white white of her summer dress as she falls.

It's a dream I have often, recurring with slight differences over the years. Maybe it's not right to call it a dream. This is the story I tout as my first memory – I might have told it to you already? This is the day my memory began. The day my mother died. I've been told about that moment so many times by so many people, I can't be sure the images belong to me. It's like pressing a memory on to an old photograph and then being told you weren't even born when the shot was taken. Memory or fiction, does it really matter? It is part of me now.

With love to you,

Daniel xx

10th November
The Studio

Dear Alice –

I probably shouldn't have done it, but the nurses are always on at me about Dad getting more 'air'. *Get him outside. Keep him as active as you can. He's not going to get any better just sitting, is he, Mr Laird?* What they don't take into account is what a fucking operation it is to move him anywhere.

Still, the weather eased today (after the last few days, a couple of degrees feels positively balmy) so I wrapped Dad up as best I could and sat him out on the lawn in one of the old garden chairs. I brought out some blankets, the radio from the kitchen, and fed him hot tea and cigarettes.

I tucked him in and, while he dozed, I wandered round our little garden enjoying the sun on my face. I haven't been out there much since I've been back, apart from walking back and forth to get the wood. There's still a crust of snow clinging to the corners of the lawn and under the shadow of the house and shrubs.

Tatty wandered out through the back door and I called to her. She sniffed at Dad, squinted at me, squatted to piss and then took herself back off inside to the fire. She works her body like a mechanical toy over the steps, rocking from front legs to back. She probably wondered why we were determined to sit out in what she considers her toilet. I could see a litter of frozen turds punctuating the grass. Avoiding them, I made my way over to the pool.

The pool is really little more than a deep pond. You've probably heard about it, and certainly you've seen it – it's what he used for the Submerged Nude series. Sarah was the primary model for that series. In fact it was her arrival that inspired the digging of the pool, and her comfort that inspired the dangerous collection of heating pipes Dad installed under the water. He always made sure the power was off before she got in. There even used to be fish in there at one point, Sarah would blame any twitches or movement on the shock of their rushed scuffs against her ankles. Not that Dad ever allowed excuses. She would work in there until her fingers and toes were puckered and white, Dad glowering down at her from that stepladder contraption he used. It was my job to hold the ladder still and then be ready with robe and towels for Sarah's breaks, to smooth soft cotton over her shuddering limbs.

It's all overgrown now, with great tufts of grass and a hazel sapling clinging bravely to the far bank. What can be seen of the muddy water is iced over and speckled with yellow bubbles, some poor drowned rodent upended with its claws and snout thrust through the ice. You'd never guess the depths. Maybe the fish are still there, slowly revolving in the dark.

I stubbed out my cigarette and roused Dad. Tatty came out again to check on us and I snapped a couple of pictures of them for Mab. Then I sat down and tried to get some conversation going over today's crossword. But Dad just sat there, staring straight ahead, tugging and tweaking the blankets on his lap. He works his mouth around sounds, but I can't make out any actual words. I was beginning to wish I hadn't woken him, and started filling in the blanks with an approximation of his jabber.

'That's right, Dad. Seven letters, BASMUNDT. That would make five across WHASTHAYA. Excellent work.

'By Jove, two down, he's got it in one. How could I have missed that?'

I got quite a kick out of it. My laughter seemed to catch something and he looked at me. Blankly at first and then he started up gurgling, right down at the back of his throat. His mouth hung open and tears rolled down the side of his flushed face. My father, remembering how to laugh.

I don't know why he had to be so sad about it?

(Later)

You remind me of Sarah. Of course she never had the advantage of your hair, but there are similarities. I hadn't wanted to admit it before now. I wanted our memories to be ours, but I keep tangling your image up in events that happened years before I met you. I think that has to be because you look like her.

Picturing your face,

Daniel xx

12th November
The Studio

Dear Mab –

The nurse came today, so Tatty and I took to the road.

She really does hate me, you know. I'm too big to be ordered into place. I find myself seeking out corners when she arrives. I lurk under the slope of the stairs, trying to control my breathing – I take in too much air – and feel my eyes work as I follow her progress around the room. It's better not to be there.

When we got back from our walk her car was still there. I let Tatty strain her lead as I knocked the butt of my cigarette out on the sole of my shoe and tried to untangle my scarf. The window was open and there was the murmur of conversation. Two voices. My name. Her name. The old story.

They shut up as soon as I opened the door and turned, their lips wet and parted. The pretty nurse made a fuss of Tatty, as Maggie gathered up cups of half-drunk tea. Maggie must have told her I was nothing to be afraid of, or else she was proving something to herself.

Dad dozed in his chair under a layer of fresh bandages. 'Must be getting on,' snapped between the two women like conspiratorial kisses. Neither of them met my eye. The nurse was gone and Maggie in the kitchen and I stood there with Tatty's lead still in my hand, blocking the light.

Still here,

Daniel

15th November
The Studio

Dear Alice –

My sister sent me a mask. Apparently she reads the letters I send her and something I wrote inspired her. It arrived this morning, all the way from Corsica, wrapped in brown paper and plastic with a card. It really is a horrible thing.

It's a full face of unpainted white clay, tumbled under her hands until it's smooth as a river stone. The forehead and cheekbones are exaggerated and swell obscenely above the dainty chin, with holes gouged out for eyes and mouth. I propped it up on my father's desk and let it survey the room.

Mab had fixed it with a leather strap like a thin belt, with a buckle on the back. It is meant to be worn. And worn by me. Mab only makes masks to order, and even then only when she feels something from the people who are ordering. God only knows where she gets the money to be so fussy, but it seems to do nothing to lessen the demand for her work. Quite the contrary, in fact. But from what I remember of her workshop her masks are usually bright – even gaudy – affairs. This is quite a departure for her.

It took me a while to psych myself up to putting the thing on. It sat on the desk while I completed my morning tasks. Dad, of course, didn't notice it, but I found I was very aware of its blank presence on the desk. In the end I gave in and took it through to the bathroom. I sat down on the toilet to fit it on to my face. I remembered Mab telling an acting coach, for whom she was making a batch of 'characters', how important it was to take the time to inhabit the mask before you look in the mirror.

I am blinkered by the mismatch of my eyes and the holes in the mask. I am forced to stare straight ahead to find light. The mask is heavy, pulling my head forward and my shoulders up. I am being reshaped. Unbidden, my tongue creeps out through the crevice of the mouth and explores its edges. The clay snatches the moisture from my tongue and I taste dust and the sweat from my sister's fingers. I cannot resist the mirror. I lumber towards it on bent knees. Two steps that are not my own.

You cannot see a mask until you're inside it. I am the jelly behind the hard clay, but it's the clay that breathes. Damp stains around the hole Mab has plucked for his mouth are all that is left of me. That, and a wet glister of life in the shadow of the eyes. I am swallowing the taste of him along with the look. The dust and the sweat and the tweak of the piggy nose and the troughs and peaks of that horrible face are in my body; in my stomach; in the shift of my feet.

And I recognise him. That monster in the mirror. Just as she said I would. That's what she wrote on the back of the postcard.

Dad was shifting about in the other room and Tatty took up barking to alert me. I slipped off the mask and stood for a moment, startled by my own face in the mirror, before I went to settle Dad back into his chair. I watched my hands as I brewed tea. I am altogether too pink and pliable; my edges are ill-defined.

I'd left the mask face-down on the toilet seat, a harmless curve of clay with its leather strap unbuckled. I had to move it when I brought Dad through. I thought about smashing it. I thought about sending it back to Mab. I thought about smashing it and then sending it back. But I hung it above my bed instead. There was a nail there, waiting for a picture, or a crucifix.

Mab's card went in the wood burner. I don't keep her postcards any more.

Daniel xx

17th November
The Studio

Dear Aubrey –

There is no need to worry about me. Please. I am not one of your pathetic patients; I do not need to be examined. Trust you to overreact to that letter. It's stuff and nonsense. An old story about an old man who couldn't cope with life – not much of a Miracle to my mind. I just thought it might amuse you.

Not to say I was exactly laughing, but I have no need to call you into action. Things have changed, Aubrey. You are no longer in control of my life; it's time to accept that.

And stop the threats to contact my sister. We do not need your input. And anyway, she can't stand you.

Daniel

17th November
The Studio

Dear Alice –

Why did you ever come to Aubrey? That's a question I would be too afraid to ask you to your face. I know you will feel you explained yourself in session, but you'd be surprised how elusive the answers are in the notes I receive from Aubrey. He does his best, but they miss so much of the body language, nuance and mode of expression. Is it really possible to ever understand someone from words on a page? I suppose that is what I am fated to be for you, for the time being at least.

Oh, Alice, there were so many women I met on pages in Aubrey's short cribbed hand. So many tales of woe, of disappointment and regret. But only one of those women I fell in love with. There is no need to be jealous. You are the only one who sang from the page. To think of me, typing up the first session. Such a routine task, conducted in the corner of Aubrey's living room, in the dusty alcove he laughingly called my study. It was there then, that magic. It was as if life was being breathed into me again after long absence. After long abstinence. I was in love again.

I met Aubrey through my sister. Did I ever tell you that? It had been a dark time for me and I'd escaped to Mab's island to recuperate. Strange to think of that summer in Corsica, while sitting here now in the place I had escaped from. From the smell of oils and turpentine to the wet earth of Mab's studio, all seemingly in a moment. The long glare of light which was that summer.

For the first weeks I lay in a darkened bedroom, twisting in the slight breeze through cotton curtains; listening to Freya's laughter and games in the garden below, her hushed whispers at my door. The strange gloomy uncle who appeared in the night, to be met by a bright young niece. A niece he'd never heard so much as a whisper of from his secretive sister. Later, they limped me out to a chair in that garden, dry dust and sun; Freya bringing me insects and oddities to discover, dropping them in my shrouded lap and then scampering away. Later again, a boat trip. Casting off from a sun-drenched city, peopled by tourists and the silent houses of the dead. The cliffs wept water and Freya took my hand. Mab took photographs and I grinned for the camera, all gums.

Later that week, Aubrey arrived. He wore his three-piece suit to the studio – of course – and sweated and fretted about the transfer of muck and dust, constantly wiping his hands and forehead with a white handkerchief. They fed me the idea that he had some plan for the use of masks in therapy. I wasn't to know he had been invited.

Aubrey is an old 'friend' of Mab's mother, Eleanor Laird. For 'friend' read ex-lover. He's one of the few men I've ever seen Mab make time for. Though I can't understand why. Oh, he was all smiles and self-deprecating wiles to Freya and me. But, when someone's in the business of making masks, they see through them quickly enough, and Mab made short shrift of his bluster. I'm sure she splattered that expensive suit with wet clay on purpose – she certainly didn't apologise – but her laugh didn't have the cruel edge I was expecting. Maybe I'm underestimating her. Maybe she was really just desperate to see me gone.

Still, when Aubrey emerged spattered and stained from her studio, Mab announced he would be staying for a few days. By time we sat down in the garden with cold glasses of champagne and nothing to toast, the plot was afoot.

'Your sister tells me you have an interest in my field.'

'I've never really thought about it.'

'Oh, it's fascinating. Constant challenge. Constant diversity. Constant change.' He beat out his points, manicured nails on a tailored thigh. 'And the things you learn. Remarkable what people will tell you. How much they are willing to invest in the process.'

'Don't you have to have training?'

'Well, yes, of course. But at my advanced age it would be helpful to have some fresh perspective.' He leant towards me. Maybe he was already a little drunk. 'And in return I can show you my work. I'm talking about serious work within the interpretative process. A way of gaining true understanding.'

We sat for a moment, watching Mab and Freya play in the dry shrub and listening to the bubbles crack against the surface of the wine.

'Women are my field really. I mean that I don't take any male clients. It's all about women for me. Mab told me you were interested in women?'

Well, how did he expect a boy of barely sixteen to answer that question? Of course I was interested in women! Well, it has always been one woman at a time for me, my darling, as you know.

Oh, Alice, I was so vulnerable and Aubrey was so clever. It was then that he sold me his grand idea. As if, spontaneously, it had struck him, there in the garden. I was to return to Manchester and work with him. He even flattered me that my last name, with its 'artistic associations', would be of use to him.

I suppose – and I know this may sound like more psychological claptrap – I was in need of a father. Mine had so rudely cast me from his life. So violently. And here was this avuncular chap, round and neatly cut as one of Mab's characters. He was perfect. And I was weak.

And so, I let myself become his toy son. His private patient and glorified secretary, who added a name of note to his flyer, and was on hand to type up the sorrows of the poor wretches who couldn't resist him.

Not that you were anything like the rest of them, my darling. You were, and are, remarkable.

I've noticed that things with Aubrey have changed since arriving here. Or maybe they've changed since I met and fell in love with you? I am no longer the child to be taken care of. You have taught me how to be an adult.

Your Daniel x

20th November
The Studio

Dear Mab –

Strange how what I've been taking for activity can so easily be pointed out to be idleness. I'd just got back from the supermarket and was hauling bags into the kitchen where I found Maggie waiting for me.

'You took your time.'

'And hello to you. Thanks for watching Dad; how's he been?'

'It's no good, this, Daniel. You need to sort the place out. I can't be here every hour of the day cleaning up after the pair of you. I've my own family to take care of.'

'I'm sorry. Look, I got Dad some new trousers. They're jogging bottoms, so we can pull them on and off more easily, and they were cheap so we don't need to worry about accidents. Where did these flowers come from? What are they, lilies? We always seem to have fresh flowers and I'm not buying them. Don't give me that look, Maggie, I'm really sorry. Maybe I should have brought you some flowers?'

'Oh, don't you come it with the hugs and kisses. You're not a little boy any more. You need to get this house right for your dad. You've got no work to go to and nothing else to do, as far as I can see. It's not right, a grown man sat about the house smoking all day. You need to make yourself useful.

'First things first. You need to get a bed down here for him. He's been sleeping on that chair for months now, after he filled that boxroom upstairs with clutter. You can get him one of those beds down from the attic room. Mabel's old wire-spring should be still packed up there in bits. And I should know: it was me that packed the bloody thing in the first place.

'Now don't you go disappearing down those bags – I can see to putting this lot away and you can make a start. I'll give you a shout before I leave. See how much you can get done before then. Might even be a cup of tea in it for you.'

So I was set to my task. When will she remember that she isn't actually our mother? I stamped up the stairs like a truculent teenager. Then I faced the attic. It's going to take me at least a week to clear. Dad seems to have been using it as a dumping ground since I left.

Our little sleeping den under the rafters. Do you remember it, Mab? You must. It's our childhoods that are packed away in that room. Our memories.

(Later)

If they are our memories, then how come I don't remember any of them? There are toy planes and a doll's house, for Christ's sake! I'm going to have to hire a skip for all this crap. I'll send you the receipt in my next letter.

(Later)

You will not believe what I found in the attic. Maggie's Tarot pack. Well, parts of it. Do you remember that summer she tried to convince us she was a gypsy? Massive Maggie, the butcher's daughter, decked out in dangly earrings, fringed scarves and long skirts, whispering fortunes to us in our cots. You, of course, too tall for yours and too wise for either me or Maggie.

'It's unlucky,' you told her. 'You shouldn't buy a Tarot pack, you have to steal them.'

'Maggie Cotton is no thief. And I'll have you know these cards are a family heirloom, passed down through the generations.'

We could hear her struggling with the cellophane wrapping. In fact, I'd been with her the day before when she bought them in the hippie shop that had just opened up in town. She'd let me get a pack of joss sticks. I broke them up and used them to pretend to smoke. The attic stank of patchouli.

'You can have one card each and then to sleep. No, Mabel, do it properly. Take it with your left hand, like it says to in the book.'

She sat down heavily on my feet and fanned the cards for you. The Fool. I sniggered.

'Shut up, idiot.'

'No, the Fool is a good card. Now, let me see,' Maggie opened the book that came with the cards, careful not to crack the spine. 'Here we go: adventure and travel; new starts and new beginnings.'

'I like the dog.'

'Now it's Danny's turn.'

'This is stupid,' you said, but I saw you slip the Fool under your pillow.

I chose the Lovers and you laughed at me. I was embarrassed, but was too young to know why. Maggie was sweet to me, telling me whatever fortune they had written down; stroking my hair. My bones rocked as she shifted her haunches.

'Plenty of time for all that when you're a big boy.'

But I knew I was already a big boy. They were always telling me so at school.

She left me with the card and eventually I stole yours. Did you know that? They're not with the pack I found, but I can still remember the faces.

The Lovers were a pair of figures in courtly dress and would not meet my eye, so absorbed were they by each other's. The man had long hair, almost as long as the woman's. Their faces were so alike, they could have been transferred one from the other. A naked cherub hung from the branches of the trees that twined around them and aimed its dart at their linked hands as if to cut them in two.

Your Fool's moonlike face gazed wistfully towards a decorative border, where bolts of gold paint were twisted into the assumption of a sun. The little mongrel dog appeared in the bottom right-hand corner, his jaws agape, seeming ready to nip at the heels of his master and frighten him off the cliff-edge that threatened his feet. That's what you'd liked; that's what you'd thought was funny.

They were such treasures to me at one time. I would look at them every night you were away. They must be somewhere in all this mess. Perhaps, if I had been a normal boy, I would have had a treasure chest of some kind. A tobacco tin bound up in rubber bands and tape, which I buried in the garden, like those time capsules they have on TV, for other kids to find and wonder at. Perhaps, if I had been a normal boy, I would understand more about the contents of this room than a shabby pack of cheap Tarot cards.

I haven't even found the beds yet.

I enclose a letter for Freya.

Daniel

P.S. Thank you for the present. I'm still not sure what to make of it. I've hung it over my bed until I decide.

20th November
The Studio

Dear Freya –

Thank you for your letter. And I must apologise for mine. You must be sick of comments like this, but – for me, in my head – you will always be that little girl who scratched at the door of my sick room in Corsica, ready to play and always asking for another game. But now I must think of you as an elegant young lady of fifteen. This makes me feel about a hundred years old.

I'm more than happy to be an excuse for you to use your written English – which is excellent, by the way. This is another thing I can't imagine: you and your mother chatting away in French. She was always hopeless at languages at school. Believe me, I've seen the reports.

Your grandad is doing fine. I'm sure your mum will explain better than I can, but he's not up to writing just yet. I did read him your letter and I'm sure he was as pleased as me to hear all your news, especially about your art lessons. We'd love to hear some more and I'm sure that a picture or two would really brighten up the house, if you feel like sharing. It can be pretty lonely here, with just your grandad and Tatty for company, but we're all getting on all right.

Hope to hear from you again soon,

Uncle Dan

23rd November
The Studio

Dear Alice –

Usually when people meet me it's my father they want to know about. Not you, my darling; you didn't even make the connection, did you? And now I refuse to sit here and write another letter about the great men in my life, Aubrey Tolburgh and Michael Laird. It was the women who were important. For me at least.

When I was a child, they came through the studio one by one, only occasionally in groups, rows of limbs and breasts and arses. Quite an education. I watched them as they posed and during their breaks. Some bound themselves up in robes; some paraded naked, stretching out cramps and scratching at pubic hair and armpits. Carols, Karens, Susans, Jennifers and Janes; even a Gertrude and a Heidi. Some were kind to me. Some I loved.

Katie. She was a delicate thing, with scuffed knees and long dark marks on her forearms and thighs. She said she bruised like soft fruit; that it was nothing to worry about. She was so slight that my father had to force her into complicated and painful poses to get some sense of undulation.

'What do you think of when you're posing, Katie?'

'I don't know. It's a long concentration. I think about everything and nothing. Mostly just try and forget about the pain. Sing songs in my head. Make lists of what I have to do.'

'I think about the ways I'll put your father to death if he doesn't give me the break he promised.' That was another

one. There was a group of girls gathered round the kitchen table with cups of tea and cigarettes. They laughed at the other girl's comment, but I wanted to hear more from Katie. I wanted to hear the right answer to my question: that, when she modelled, she thought of me.

Katie was one of the first girls he submerged. This was before Sarah arrived and the pool was dug; Katie had to make do with the downstairs bath and Dad hanging over the shower rail. Her dark hair was so thin you could see segments of white scalp between the wet locks. That night, I lay in the same bath, the tack tack of my fist familiar against the perfumed water as I brought myself off, to thoughts of Katie lowering her bony behind on to my cock, my fingers gripping and marking her pale flesh with bruises my father would have to paint in the next day.

I bumped into Victoria ('call me Vicky') in the village shop yesterday. She was another of the local girls, now married with children in high school ties by her side and a basket full of sweet breakfast cereal and fizzy drinks. I managed to ask after Katie and she told me she'd disappeared to the city with a bad lot after Dad stopped booking her. I was grateful that, after the first shock of recognition, I could remember I never much cared for Victoria. She looked old and faded and seemed annoyed, even nervous, at meeting me. You'd think she'd be grateful for the distraction, for the chance to relive better days.

Maggie was the one that never left. She was the mother hen with the frying pan at the stove, distributing tea and cigarettes, laughing, and chiding the girls who complained about the poses they'd been set, the length of time they'd been forced to sit, the large boy who followed them about and destroyed their concentration. Maggie would hear no criticism of me, and those models who dared it had short careers in the Laird studio. Dad was famous enough by that time; there would always be more girls. Until there was Sarah, of course. And then there was only Sarah.

For me, now it will only be you.

Your Daniel x

27th November
The Studio

Dear Aubrey –

You'll probably have a hundred reasons in a file somewhere to explain why I'm saying this, but really, Aubrey, you must take this as my final word: I have no use for more of your pills. Your letters, however, I have to admit are welcome. It's good to have someone objective to write to; someone who's not tied up in the emotional stuff going on here.

I've been thinking a little lately about our relationship. Maybe sometimes I am unfair to you. I blame you for not playing a part, and I'm not even sure anyone informed you that we were on stage.

I'm with Dad at the hospital for his check-up. Isn't everyone meant to say they hate hospitals? I have to say I don't mind them. I find the waiting rather restful. There's the smell, of course – sanitised wards imbued with the stench of stewed shit – but it just makes it more intimate, like using a toilet when the seat's still warm.

We wait with the very old. I try to mimic the other carers with their loud whispered questions and concerns. It's hard to keep Dad in his chair. He keeps twitching his fingers against the armrests and then trying to haul himself up. I don't know where else he thinks he needs to be, but, wherever it is, he wants to get there in a hurry. I'm getting kind of pissed off with him, but one of the other carers gives me a smile-grimace of sympathy and I'm forced to play the dutiful son. I get Dad a magazine and turn the pages of glossy smiles under his chin, trying to catch his attention. I'm like a child with a buttercup: *do you like butter?* What I want to do is just sit here and watch the nurses and the doctors and the patients. I want to be ignored by the women busy behind their desks and carry a chit of paper from the blue waiting room to the red waiting room. I want to follow the biro lines round every completed word search and drink overpriced watered-down coffee in the cafeteria. I could live here quite happily for months. I realise I'm hoping they'll say that Dad's too bad to go home, that we'll get a little holiday in the hospital.

The doctor says he's progressing well, but slowly. He says Dad's speech still isn't great, but he does have some words now, which should cut down on the frustration and tantrums. He mentions small strokes occurring all the time. Landmines in his brain. He reads all this off a clipboard after greeting Dad and taking hold of his hand. He lets Dad keep hold of his hand while he reads. Dad is very quiet. He watches the doctor's face. I find myself embarrassed by the fact that the doctor is talking to me and not Dad. I also worry Dad's about to say something. He has that look more and more these days, as if he's just going to come out and say it: 'I hate this man. This is the son I hate. This is the son I had to beat nearly to death to get out of my house. This is who you have taking care of me. Who you have living with me. Help me.'

But he doesn't say anything, just twists his mouth and watches the doctor talk. I notice how dirty Dad's glasses are, and the stains on his trousers. I should have dressed him up for the doctor. I should be doing a better job. If I do a better job, maybe when the time comes he'll forgive me for whatever it was I did so wrong.

Daniel

28th November
The Studio

Dear Mab –

I've been digging into the attic for days now and I finally reached your bed. Maggie was right, it was packed into pieces, and piled on top of it were canvases. New paintings. I'm not talking about a few pieces here, Mab. There are over twenty – and that's not counting the sketches. The weirdest thing is: they are all portraits. They're obviously Dad's work, but I've never seen them before. Do you know anything about them?

Whoever stored them here couldn't have cared much about the condition they would be found in. They've been piled face to face, so the oils have to be peeled free of each other, leaving eyes and ears and lip smears on the face of their partner. Some I'm too scared to touch, they're so bound together and dried into place.

There are three subjects: me, Sarah, and Dad himself. When could he have painted these? Oh, why do I ask you that question, when we both know when he must have done it?

But, they're good, Mab. Really good. I think they must be some of his best work. And they are so different from the Nudes series. It's not just that they're portraits; the quality of brushwork and the insight is exquisite. They are like nothing I've ever seen before. But they are definitely Dad's.

It was right at the bottom of the pile that I found the self-portraits. I have one propped in front of me while I write. He must have used several mirrors, because he doesn't meet the eye. (In fact, thinking about it, most of the subjects are looking away into the far corners of the paintings… that old life model trick about never meeting the artist's eye.) I know how you feel about self-portraits, but there's none of that strained intensity you hate so much. He just looks as if he's sitting there thinking about something, as if he's watching TV. There's a cigarette in his hand rather than a brush, and his glasses show a film of grime and slight reflections of the light from the window. There's no trace of vanity in this painting; you can see the marks of age, the old man he is becoming. No paint-splattered clothing or easel intersecting the canvas; no painful landmarks to his trade. He is just another subject to be examined.

We have to do something with these paintings, Mab. Even if it is to burn them.

Daniel

59

30th November
The Studio

Dear Mab –

The first thing I noticed was that a handful of grape hyacinths had joined the red tulips in the vase on the mantelpiece. More fresh-cut flowers. I never usually notice flowers, but they've been invading our house in various forms over the past few months, everything from stargazer lilies to dead nettles in a jam jar. Maggie has dodged any questions about them, but I suppose I just assumed it was her bringing them in. They never lasted long enough to wither; their water was always clean and fresh. Who wouldn't think that was Maggie?

Tatty didn't react any differently, just shook her ragged coat as I unhooked the lead and did her usual stumbling run towards Dad's chair.

'Hello, Daniel.'

It was Sarah. I didn't recognise her. How ridiculous is that? Even after staring at her portraits only a few days before. This was the meeting I've been waiting for half my life and all I could find to say was, 'I thought you were the district nurse.'

'I just popped in to see how Michael was doing. I was only here for Michael. I should be going.'

She was gathering up bags at her feet and paused to make a small fuss of Tatty's head. I could see the grey hair threaded through the blonde, like white wires. She looked up. Her skin looked thicker. She'd put on weight. She was still beautiful.

'I didn't know you were still in the area.'

My voice worked its way out of my mouth, but I could barely understand the words. I just knew I had to keep her here. Now I'd found her, I couldn't just let her leave.

'Oh, I'm not. Not any more. I was just passing, you know.' She leant over to kiss Dad, smoothing the wisps of hair down on to his scalp with a passing hand. Her bags were on her shoulder and she just stood there gripping their straps, not meeting my eye. 'I should go.'

'Those nurses, you know, they're always changing them. I never know who I'm going to come home to. Tatty hasn't taken too well to the latest set, so I take her out. We've been down by the allotments, sniffing at the hedgerows. Tatty, not me. Though I did pick these sloes; Maggie mentioned she might use them to make some gin. Do you remember that year we made sloe gin?'

This went on for some time; I can't tell you for how long, but my mouth kept moving and the words kept falling out. I said anything just to keep Sarah in the room. I told her about the different nurses, including the one who hates me, and about my walks with Tatty and about Dad and what the doctors had said. I fished memories from somewhere, not all of them happy, and threw them into the space between us. I willed her to interrupt me; to smile or react; to come a little closer; to look at me.

Then Maggie pushed the door open behind me, startling my heels. She stood in the doorway a moment and surveyed the room.

'You're all here, then.' Nothing surprises Maggie. I don't think I ever seen her expression change. 'I've brought back your washing.'

'I was just leaving,' Sarah said.

61

'Hello there, Michael. Had your visitor for the day?'

'My car is just outside. I stayed a bit longer than I should.'

'That's right. You get going and Daniel here can make me and his dad a cup of tea. I've been on my feet since six. You got everything, love?'

'Sarah and I were just… I got in and she was here. You can stay for a cup of tea, can't you, Sarah?'

'Now, Danny, don't bother the girl. She's had her visit and now she's on her way. Now get into that kitchen. I'll make sure she gets off all right.'

I saw her smile at Maggie and give one look back at Dad, but I didn't see her leave.

Maggie refused to tell me anything about the visits – I had gathered by now that they had been going on for some time along with their accompanying flowers. She refused to talk to me about Sarah at all. She does this thing when I ask a question she doesn't like, where she turns to either Dad or the dog and begins a conversation.

'You enjoying that tea there, Michael?'

'Have a good walk today, did you, girl?'

'You two have any idea what nonsense this lad is talking?'

Simple, but impenetrable.

I divided the flowers and placed half of them in a clean tooth mug by my bed. With your mask hanging above them, it looks rather like an altar. I wonder what it is I'm worshipping.

Daniel

1st December
The Studio

Dear Aubrey –

I apologise for the call last night. I just found myself walking – there was no chance of sleep – and then I was inside the phone box by the village shop and scrabbling for change. I had to talk to someone and you were the only one I could call. I'm sorry the hour was far from convenient, but there was no need to be quite so dismissive.

I need your help, Aubrey. I dealt with the whole Sarah situation so badly – I was so raw and obvious. After all the work we have done, I just fell apart at the sight of her. I need to make a plan – or should I say *we* need to make a plan – for the next encounter. I wrote a hasty note to Mab last night and found I was unable to recall all that was said. Can you believe that? After all my hours scripting for you. And yet in that meeting with Sarah there are blanks – utter blanks – just the memory of a quivering childish panic, a weakness in the knees and the distinct need to urinate. I was still shaking for an hour after she left.

I know you have a pill for this – I know I've refused them a thousand times – but what I'm saying now is, send me some!

I am a failure, Aubrey.

Perhaps it would be worth investing in some kind of recording device, seeing as my brain has deserted me. I could fix something up with Dad's old stereo in the sitting room, if I could just get my hands on a microphone. But then there would still be the physical signals to record. Maybe a video camera – they make those pretty small these days? You must know about this stuff; you have to have been using something like it since I left.

I'm relying on you, Aubrey. Just tell me what to do. I expect her every moment; at every turn of the door. It's terrible. I daren't leave the house in case she comes again.

Awaiting your reply,

Daniel

3rd December
The Studio

Dear Mab –

A calmer day. Instead of leaving the house, I have finally finished clearing the attic. The portraits, I have put in the studio. I've arranged them as best I can, trying to get some idea of sequence. Occasionally I've caught myself going up to look at them. And not just the ones of Sarah; there's some fascination in staring into your own face, viewed through the eyes of another. If *fascination* is the right word. Maybe better to say it's *mesmerising*. I'm not sure what to make of the expressions depicted. I can't quite read them. It's like staring at a text in a language very close to your own, but still impenetrably foreign. Does that make sense?

Your old bed has been set up downstairs for Dad. Clean white sheets and banked up with pillows by Maggie, it's a little slice of hospital living. Dad hates being moved out of his chair and into bed in the evening – especially after a few glasses of whisky – but I've been making him do it.

Saying that, Maggie complained about finding him in his day clothes when she got him up this morning. I've been putting him in jogging bottoms and sweatshirts from the supermarket – they can be washed easily and even thrown away if they get too stained or acquire too many cigarette burns – and couldn't see the point in going through the fuss of changing him before bed. I have enough trouble with the morning wash and change. Anyway, once he's tucked under the white blankets, you can't tell. He looks like the perfect patient. Maggie's just in a bad mood about me passing her the dog-walking duties.

I've been finding it tough to sleep, but my files have proved a great consolation. I am able to see now where I went wrong in the meeting with Sarah. I simply let the emotion of the occasion overwhelm me. I typed out the scene as best I could on Dad's old typewriter. It was like being back at work. I even drew out a small floor plan. Such a small room, it manages to look cluttered as I place people into it. Of course at the time Maggie's little occasional tables were still in place with their mouldering houseplants. They've all, thankfully, found their way into the skip now. But I find I'm rather sad to see them go, the fringe of dried leaves which stood between Sarah and me. We were so close. I must have brushed past her on my way through to the kitchen, but I have no memory of it.

There is a point to all this, the element I completely neglected to take into account: Dad.

After so many weeks here, I think I've started to regard him, not as a threat, but as a list of tasks to be completed. It's only recently that he's even begun to talk – and most of that doesn't make sense – but imagine the effect he must have had on Sarah. Seeing me come through the door with Dad sitting by her side, she must have been terrified for me. Don't you see, Mab, this explains everything: Sarah's reticence and the tension in the room, which affected me so disastrously. Now I just have to figure out a way of getting Dad out of the house before her next visit. After what she witnessed on my last day here, after what she saw him do to me, no wonder she was scared. If only Dad were as easy to remove as dying houseplants.

Awaiting your reply,

Daniel

3rd December
The Studio

Dear Freya –

I'm sorry it has taken me so long to reply to your last letter. The truth is, I don't have much news to share. Life is very slow here. Especially slow when compared to yours: you seem to have so many friends and things to do. It's quite dizzying. I had to read and reread your letter to get the names straight in my mind. Could I ask you to describe your friends a little, or even send us some pictures? I do like to have an image of the people you are writing about, and it would be lovely to see what you look like now. I know Grandad would like it too.

I did have a very old friend pay a visit. It's remarkable really, that, just by standing still for a time, someone so important can fall back into your life. Particularly when that someone has been lost for so long. You should be grateful: you are still young enough not to have experienced a loss like that. Although maybe I could count as a lost person in your life? Do you even remember my visit? I suppose you must. At least you had news of me from your mother? She was always good about keeping in touch.

Do you recall my reading you stories from that fairytale book you carried around with you? The one you kept in a pink backpack full of special treasures. You were never much interested in the words, but traced the illustrations with your small fingertips and insisted that I tell you a version of the story written there in the pictures on the page. The princesses, of course, had to play the central role, but you were never happy with them lying around and waiting for Prince Charming. The women must perform the rescues and save the day. Poor Prince Charming was rather left out of things. You accepted him as a mere part of the bounty, being much more interested in the animals and the dwarves and, of course, the mother Queen.

Maybe I will be saved by my own princess coming to rescue me? I do hope so. I've always fancied myself a Prince Charming. Though it would make rather a complicated fairytale.

With much love and looking forward to your next letter,

Uncle Dan

3rd December
The Studio

Dear Alice –

I'm sorry it has been so long since I last wrote. Things continue much the same here.

Dad has developed a habit of crying at the least thing. It really is quite disturbing. As I sit here writing at the desk, he's weeping. I just brought him a cup of tea and rolled him three cigarettes, which are sitting on the arm of the chair untouched. I've emptied his catheter bag and he's had his morning wash and change.

I've even tried just squatting down by the side of his chair and holding his hand. He has beautiful hands, my father. Nothing like my stub-fingered plates. They look as though they've been carved out of close-grained wood, each tangled vein polished to a dull sheen. He's always been proud of his long, fluted nails, keeping them obsessively clean, and I noticed the lines of filth that had built up over his confinement. I busied myself digging out the dirt with the end of a wooden toothpick, until he gently tugged his hand away to press his palms against his face. The tears glittered in the light from the TV and the sobs came in long, shuddering gasps. He's been refusing to wear his glasses.

I don't know what I'm meant to do.

Daniel x

5th December
My sickbed

Dear Mab –

I am sitting on my bed, banked up by pillows, nursing a cold. There is no one to nurse me. I am full of self-pity.

Maggie has arrived to look after Dad for the afternoon. I heard her voice through the floorboards and for a moment I thought it was Sarah come again to visit. It was enough to start me out of my bed and towards the door. I must be delusional. Then Maggie gave her shout up the stairs and I scurried back to my sheets.

All for the best really: I couldn't have Sarah seeing me like this. My head is full and heavy and I ooze. A ghoul met me in the shaving mirror this morning. Not that this is enough for Maggie. She's convinced I'm faking. She even went so far as to accuse me of a night on the tiles. Some fucking chance.

The tulips by my bed have blown and their petals crystallised into contortions. Their dry stalks rattle and whisper as I shift on my bed. I won't throw them away; there is still a kind of beauty in them. More than can be said for me.

Why doesn't she come, Mab? I've been ready and waiting for days. I've even taken special care of Dad, had him up, clean and waiting with me. I've started watering down his whisky. In fact, I must warn Maggie to use the open bottle and leave the undoctored one. It's been making things easier in the morning, but more difficult at night. It takes so much longer to get him to sleep. I wondered about asking the doctor for some pills to help him sleep through?

I'm up at least once or twice every night herding him back into his cot. Thank God for Tatty, who starts yapping as soon as he starts to wander.

I'm terrified I'll pass on this cold.

Is this letter anything but nonsense? I can't tell. Maggie keeps heaving up the stairs with questions and interrupting me. She said if I'm well enough to be scribbling I should be well enough to do without her. She must have had some other plan for today. How strange it is that we know so little about what goes on in her life away from here. Is that father of hers still alive behind the boards covering the front of the butcher's shop? Why did she never marry?

(Later)

All is forgiven. I must have fallen asleep, because I woke to Maggie bringing me a tray with a bowl of tinned soup and a plate of buttered toast cut into triangles. She even pushed back my hair to feel my temperature with the back of her hand. Then she sighed and headed back downstairs. No words. Still, it is definite progress.

Daniel x

12th December
The Studio

Dear Alice –

I'm sorry this letter is late. I've been ill. What I thought was a cold turned out to be flu and had me laid up in bed for days. I had a fever. How I longed for your cool hands.

Maggie told me I spoke in my sleep; the first thing she said that I could make sense of was, 'Who's this Alice, then?'

I've been so distracted recently. Even before my illness this place infected me. I was seeing things not as the man I am, but as the boy I was when I escaped. You came to me in my fever and rescued me. I can still taste you on my lips. Milk and honey. I dread to think what I whispered to Maggie in the night.

I feel so weak and light, despite Maggie constantly calling me a 'great lump' as she helped me heave about the bed. She's had to give me sponge baths, I'm ashamed to say. Though at least now I'm strong enough to take care of the delicate areas myself.

My mind is so clear, it's as though I'm sitting with you. Like that day when we were first alone together. Darling, I'm so weak. I keep having to stop and put down the pen. But your face is so clear to me, so much better than the poor *doppelgänger* that's been haunting me lately. I have the transcript of that special day. Did you know I rushed home and made one? Oh, how my fingers trembled over the keys. But I had to have a record. Here, let me see what I can do with it:

I'm standing outside the door to the staircase that leads up to Aubrey's office. I'm smoking the fifth in a pack of cigarettes I brought especially to smoke here. I don't really want them, but it's nice to have an occupation. I'm early. I know you're still in session. But I want to be prepared. I have ironed this shirt and inspected the rest of my clothes for coffee stains. I am still not sure about this jacket. There is nothing I can do about my hair, except try to avoid my reflection in shop windows as I walked here from the bus stop.

I'm not prepared. I have no idea what I'm doing. There is no plan.

Not for the first time, I wonder at Aubrey's choice of setting for his office, but he has always had a soft spot for the Northern Quarter. I can hear his voice in my head; see him mouth the words 'soft spot'. We must have had this conversation more than once.

I smoke my cigarettes, lighting the next off the end of the last. For some reason it is important for you to meet me smoking. The street is busy, a mill of people and traffic. Something is kicking out or changing over. I am unused to it. The container that is myself is not properly sealed. I seep into the crowd, without moving from my place by the door. I allow myself to catch eyes, examine faces, and listen in to snatches of conversation. I allow myself to feel. I should know better. I have been too long confined. I have grown soft at my edges.

Maybe I am more prepared than I think I am. A girl. A shock of blonde hair. The door at my back. I had forgotten why I was here. 'I'm sorry.' Oh, why must my first words to you always be an apology?

'No, it's my – '

'No really, it was me.'

'I don't suppose you could spare one of those?'

You are standing next to me, smoking one of my cigarettes. You cough. You don't really smoke. I already know this about you.

'Are you going up?' you ask, and you look towards the window of Aubrey's office. I follow your gaze.

'No. I mean, I don't…'

'Oh, I don't mean to pry. He's very good, you know. It's difficult, isn't it? I mean, it's hard work. It *is* work. But, it's worth it. He really is very good.

'I'm Alice, by the way.'

'Daniel.'

Weren't we sweet in those first tentative days? Did you have any clue that I was already in love with you? I had no plan, but already I had decided my future was with you.

My love to you, my darling, as always,

Daniel xx

13th December
The fireside

Dear Mab –

Much stronger today. Thank you for your letter; I read some sections of it to Dad tonight in front of the fire. We both sat bundled up in blankets like old folks in their home and chuckled over your words. Well, only I chuckled, but Dad seemed to follow along all right. What are these secret plans you've got hidden up your sleeve? Are they anything to do with the portraits? It's all horribly intriguing.

Thank you for the cheque, too. I've given a little something extra to Maggie. She's been working day and night here with the pair of us on our backs. I don't know if she's found time to sleep, except for catching a few winks in Dad's chair.

I convinced her to take me out with her yesterday, when she took Tatty for a walk. We put my coat on over my pyjamas and stuffed my feet into trainers. Maggie tied my laces for me, as if I were a child being dressed for an outing. Then my feet start to work, one foot in front of the other, out of the front door, stepping over the tree roots that vein the pavement running down our street. The cracks and swells in the tarmac on display under the gloss of fresh rain.

There was rain in the air too; it washed against our faces and left us gasping. My feet were still working. I couldn't help but marvel at their dogged progress. Maggie talked to Tatty and to me, huddled deep in her raincoat; I could only catch snatches of what she said. I felt like a lunatic, stumbling alongside them with my empty head, borne onwards by my marching feet. The rain got into my eyes so I had to squint and cold leached past cuffs, waistband and neckline, penetrating my flesh in a deep shiver. My mouth formed a word and dropped it into the sharp wind that rattled our raincoats.

'What did you say?' Maggie pulled her hood to one side and stepped closer.

'Cold. I'm cold.'

'We'll get you back.'

I was glad to be able to send her home for a good night's sleep with a few notes tucked down the front of her dress.

(Later)

Dad's sleeping now, head flung back and mouth open. Giving his molars an airing. Even loading the fire doesn't disturb him, though it's an awkward business trying not to dislodge Tatty from her place on my feet. Everything's cosy tonight. Without the wretched TV blaring, we're like a sentimental painting. The kind of thing Dad always hated.

It was kind of you to offer me a break – I spared Dad that part of your letter – but to be honest I'm probably best placed here for the moment. And yes, you have that in writing! I need to get my strength back and see what I can do for the old man. Looking back over the past months, I am ashamed of the little I've actually managed to achieve. I was too busy wishing myself elsewhere. I've written to my girlfriend and she understands my position. I've made an appointment with the doctor for Monday, for me to talk to him about Dad. There has to be more we can do.

There has been no word from Sarah and I don't expect there to be. That's an old dream and I have to let it go. You weren't here when she first arrived, were you? That day when Dad came back from London with a strange girl tucked under his arm. His lifetime muse, plucked off the streets. Easy as picking a flower. I wonder what he took her from? Strange, but it never seemed to come up. It took Maggie to tell me what kind of a gift she really was; what he was really saying by bringing her here. *Here, son, here is your dead mother to play with.* 'The spit of her,' Maggie said that night, as she came in to check on me. 'It's not healthy.'

It was the next day that he started digging that pond outside. I sat eating eggs and staring at the mother I couldn't remember. Sarah drank her coffee and smiled. She asked me questions about school and put on another round of toast for me. We were so polite, sitting there at breakfast. Me in my school uniform, she in a borrowed robe and Dad outside hacking at the turf.

Dad had cut himself out, a sharp silhouette on clean white paper; you and I were the figures that folded out of him. Hand in hand we stood. The last figure, the fourth, a little ragged, a little stained, had been snipped cleanly away. So we hung either side of Dad, the blunt-cut stumps of our fingers unable to grasp. And he tacked on another. She fitted the template. What could go wrong? How could we possibly complain? We were the model family.

It's strange to stumble past the portraits lined up in the studio. Me and Sarah and Dad, all gazing to the corners of the room.

Why aren't you part of the pantomime, Mab? Whatever can it mean? Does it even matter?

Forgive this letter,

Daniel x

15th December
The Studio

Dear Aubrey –

So I phoned you during a session. You usually relish interruptions. I am your employee after all; I *should* be phoning during work hours. You complained enough when I phoned you at home. And I'll have you know I recovered from more than a simple cold. It was flu. The doctor confirmed it (and that's a real doctor, not one of your pet pharmacists). And I'm feeling much better, not that you asked. The joy I'm finding is not some passing phase or brainstorm. It's a new clarity and I'm enjoying it.

I'm sorry that I put you to the trouble of renewing my prescription, but it can hardly be a surprise to you if I look for a chemical solution when I'm desperate. It was you who taught me that was the answer. I'm sure you can put your little white pills to better use on someone else.

I had a letter from Mab today suggesting Dad and I take a short holiday to the coast. She's even sorted out a house for us. It's not far, just a couple of hours' drive. I'm going to take her up on her offer. It will do us both good to get away from this place for a while.

It means I won't be bothering you for a while. Oh, what am I saying? If you're good, I might send you a postcard.

Daniel

18th December
The Studio

Dear Mab –

We spent today packing for our holiday!

Dad's bag of clothes and bathroom gear looks so small compared to the one of assorted medical supplies. I picked those up at the doctor's the other day. I managed to get that appointment to talk to him about Dad. He was quite encouraging about the possibility of taking Dad away, but didn't have any answers about speeding up Dad's recovery. He just nodded on as I ran through what I do for him during the day. Do you think they practise those sympathetic smiles in front of a mirror?

I saved the reality of the trip until yesterday, when the nurse visited. She grumbled about the lack of notice, but conceded it was a good idea. I gathered this, of course, from her conversation with Dad. Too much to hope she might actually speak to me directly. She did accept the cup of tea I made for her, though I'm not convinced she drank it. I even felt able to stay in the house as she ministered to Dad's leg. (It's nothing serious, just a rash that built up under the catheter bag. She's given me some cream so I can treat it while we're away.)

I did catch her pushing an emergency number card into Dad's top pocket. Obviously I wasn't meant to see. Why *does* she hate me so much? Maggie, of all people, must have put her straight about the rumours.

As I packed the car, I couldn't help feeling as if we were preparing for an escape rather than a holiday. I can't be sure how much Dad knows about what's going on. I've been keeping to the regular routine as much as possible, so as not to overexcite or worry him, but actually he seems to enjoy the disruption. He followed me round the living room today as I picked up things for the trip and sat and watched me as I tried to explain what would be happening tomorrow morning. He watches so intently, like a child. He's given up even trying to speak lately, unless I refuse him a refill of his whisky or try and turn down the television.

Maybe I'm pinning too much hope on this trip. I must remember I'm packing Dad and me along with the bags. And the reason for all this careful preparation is to keep things as close to home as possible. It's just another location. *We* will still be there.

Daniel x

19th December

Dear Mab –

We have arrived at last. The chalet is simple, but perfect for us. Tatty has sniffed every corner and is now, thankfully, asleep. So is Dad. I let him have a drop of whisky in his coffee. He's yet to notice the lack of a TV.

I am happy settled in what I have decided is my chair, a book by my side, rain on the tin roof and the smell of the sea in the air. I am determined to make this work.

D.

19th December

Dear Alice –

1/3

Well, here we are, my darling. I always seem to be travelling further away from you. It is beautiful here – you'd love it. Tatty dragged me and I dragged Dad down to the beach this afternoon. What should have been a five-minute walk took us over half an hour, what with Tatty stopping to sniff every bunch of cord grass and Dad's distracted snail's pace.

D.

2/3

The tide was out. A slate-grey strip of sea against the horizon. No paddling for me. The wind was at once a beast at our backs and then roaring full into our faces. Tatty ducked behind my knees and Dad followed my footprints in the sand. Dry sand lifted and danced across the wet plains. An imitation of the water it had lost.

3/3

Dad tired quickly and it was cold. Back to chalet for warm tea and heated beans. I must shop tomorrow.

I miss you. I miss you. Huddle here with me as the rain begins to fall again. Wrap your arms around me and kiss me to sleep.

> *Loving you,*
> *Daniel x*

20th December

Dear Aubrey –

1/2

Well, I did promise you a postcard. I suppose I might owe you an apology too. I put you to trouble and you came through for me. I'd been ill. Forgive and forget that last letter of mine, won't you, old friend? And let me tell you all about my new abode.

No donkey rides or sticks of rock. The chalet's roof leaks into a bucket in the middle of the living room, where I am sleeping. At night, I am sometimes woken by a splash of water in the face. Not an arcade in sight, just a tiny village shop a ten-minute drive away, where I bought tins of food encrusted by years of dust. Not even a show at the end of the pier. No pier. You'd hate it. I love it.

D.

20th December

Dear Mab –

The weather is too bad to go out today. The wind is swallowing us and then spitting us back against the earth. Us in our little tin house, sheltering from the threat of a white Christmas.

I've started reading to Dad as a TV replacement. We're currently working on the Rex Stout omnibus I brought with me. I may look like Nero Wolfe, but I make a mean Archie Goodwin. I think Tatty appreciates it.

Dx

20th December

Dear Freya –

Your mum has treated us to a winter holiday. I took Tatty down to the beach today and watched as she got chased by the waves. She is constantly infuriated by the fact that she can't catch them in her jaws. I just hope she hasn't drunk too much seawater. Grandad, Tatty and I are curled up in front of a warm gas fire, and Tatty's coat is steaming in the heat.

    Merry Christmas!

               Uncle Dan

21st December

Dear Aubrey –

Day three by the sea. I'm trying to get Dad out as much as possible. I've set him up a folding chair outside on our little scrap of lawn and I put him out there every time the sun shows its face. We're third in a line of identical chalets, but the others are all empty. There are a couple of deluxe-looking caravans in a distant field, but I have to drive to see an unfamiliar face.

               D.

22nd December

Dear Mab –

I packed a couple of Dad's sketchbooks and today I pressed one into his hands along with a piece of charcoal as he sat in our little garden blinking at the sun. I got myself a chair and sat next to him, pretending to read the paper. I don't know what I expected. No, that's a lie. But the poor old bugger can't even change a TV channel. He dawdled the charcoal over the paper a while, until it slipped from his fingers on to the wet grass. I saved the page though. The latest work by the great Michael Laird. I hope it survives, I forgot to pack any fixative.

Dx

22nd December

Dear Alice –

I left Dad sleeping today, and went for a walk with Tatty. An excuse to dream of you a little. It's strange to be so crowded in this lonely place. You haunted me today. I kept expecting to find you coming over the next dune. Tatty set off tracking something and I was convinced it was you. I followed her for what felt like miles over the undulating and empty dune, chasing your face.

Dx

22nd December

Dear Mab –

Disaster today. Dad had a fall in the bathroom. I don't even know what he was doing in there, except that sometimes he forgets he's wearing the catheter and tries to go for a piss. His skin is like paper and he tore open his leg on something. There was a lot of blood, but when I got him cleaned up there wasn't much to it. Nothing worth cutting the trip short for.

D.

22nd December

Dear Alice –

Spent my evening painting the mouth of an angry wound on my father's leg with antiseptic. I was terrified he might need stitches. Had visions of driving to Accident and Emergency with Dad laid out on the back seat. Think it should heal up all right once it's dried.

Strange: in some places he has great folds of the stuff, but in others he barely has enough skin to cover him.

Dx

23rd December

Dear Mab –

Dad much better. Managed to cobble together a dressing. Felt safe enough to leave him for an hour so I could give Tatty a run by the sea. Their needs are better dealt with separately.

The sea surprised me: it had clawed its way up the sand and shingle and our beach had become a heaving, living thing. Tatty yapped at the waves and dodged their flowing skirts. The sound was remarkable; Tatty was no match for it. The wind chased wave-song deep into my ears. I can still hear it.

D.

23rd December

Dear Alice –

I can't believe we've only been here four days. And, in another way, I can't believe we've been here four days. Time has left us here at the edge of everything. A walk today alone. I found a small hamlet of hunkered-down cottages and a church with a ruined tower. It was open, and I found myself sitting in a pew looking at coloured glass and thinking, of course, of you.

Dx

24th December

Dear Aubrey –

More rain and again we're contained in our places round the gas fire. Dad is ill-tempered, picking at the bandages on his leg and hollering at Tatty if she tries to get near him. Merry Christmas Eve to me!

Do you think it's possible to take a holiday from yourself? Jesus, look who I'm asking!

D.

3rd January 2006

Dear Mab –

I'm so sorry, but I had to do it. I just couldn't face going back to the Studio. I suppose I reached my limit. There are so many other ways I could have left, I know.

I was just driving to the nearest shop for bread and milk. The radio was on and I was singing along to some pop tune and beating out time on the steering wheel, as I wound through single-lane roads with damp clumps of grass bursting their central seam. Then the road resolved into two lanes and then there was motorway being licked up under my tyres. I don't know when I decided I wouldn't stop, that I'd just keep driving. I know it was dark when I phoned Maggie and told her to pick up Dad and Tatty from the chalet, but I can't have left him alone for more than a few hours.

I know he's all right. That was the one thing Maggie would tell me when she rang back. I also know you must all hate me right now. But you must have known. Every letter I wrote to you was telling you this would happen. I'm sorry for the upset I've caused, but I can't say that I'm sorry I did it.

Daniel

Dear Mab –

It didn't take you long to track me down. Yes, I am holed up at Aubrey's. I should have known he'd sell me out straight away. And no, I'm not coming back. I'm needed here, Mab, and I need to be here. Aubrey has given me my job back in the 'office'.

Well, I say that; actually he said I could only have my room back if I worked for it. I'm writing this between writing-up sessions. There has been quite a backlog built up in my absence.

You needn't worry about Aubrey betraying your confidence in him. He's been giving me hell. If it were up to him, I'd be swallowing pills like sweets and spending my few conscious hours laid out on his couch revealing my deepest desires to his willing ears. Just like old times. Either that or he'd have me hog-tied and posted back to Dad's to please you. Anything to regain a little control.

Though, I think he must be secretly pleased to see me. He *has* let me stay, and – unless he's grinding them into my tea – he's letting me stay medication-free. I just have to put up with the constant 'chats' about my future and my past. If that's not torture, I don't know what is.

My main problem is my present. My Alice. I've been having trouble getting hold of her. She's cancelled her sessions with Aubrey, as I suggested, but now she's not answering her phone. I've tried to talk to Aubrey about it, but all he did was mutter jargon about relapses and destructive behaviour and then offer a brightly coloured tome from his self-help library. I have to see her and make sure she's all right. I worry my disappearance has taken a greater toll on her than she's liked to admit. She is, after all, vulnerable. How else would Aubrey have got his hooks into her? I hate to think she might be angry with me. That this is all some elaborate punishment for abandoning her for so long.

I know this must be hard for you to understand. You won't believe either of us could have feelings this strong after knowing each other for such a short time. But there's something remarkable about Alice and my relationship with her. I haven't felt this way about anyone since Sarah. Believe my feelings are as strong now as they were then and you'll have some idea how serious I am.

I've been to the Art Gallery, and the bookshop where Alice works. I'm going to her house tonight. I'm stocking up on clichés: flowers, chocolates, and pleas in the night. I'm willing to be whatever she wants me to be, if only she'll forgive me. Do you know I even feel a little shy about seeing her again? I know I'm being ridiculous, but we've communicated by letter for so long I'm scared she's become accustomed to me as words on a page. Words seem so small and elegant compared to the great hulk of me looming in her doorway.

Oh, I wish you could meet her, Mab. Then maybe you'd understand. After I first met her at Aubrey's, I went down to the bookshop to see her at work. She was so sweet and tender with the customers and their quiet purchases. I watched her slot books on to the shelves and press coins in change into the palms of a dozen strangers. Once I thought she spotted me, then I saw her cry silently when an old man came in and asked for a book. For an hour she danced between a table of paperbacks and the till, arranging a stack of new publications into a perfect spiral of spines. She pretended not to see me there and not to recognise me when I finally summoned the courage to make a purchase. But her smile was all for me, I'm sure, as she muddled about for a paper bag for my book. The type of bag they drop oranges into on the grocer's stall on Church Street.

Leave me be, Mab, I'm just trying to be happy.

Daniel

10th January
Manchester

Dear Alice –

Darling, where are you? I've tried your work and your house. I even tried phoning the emergency numbers in your file. I couldn't get any answer.

It's strange to be back, but it's even stranger to be here without you. I got off the bus by the library and walked through to Albert Square, gave the poor prince a salute where he stood, still encased in his tower of scaffolding, and sat on a bench a while and watched the people go by. I couldn't help thinking how nice it would be to sit there with you under my arm. How I wouldn't even notice the damp wood of the bench underneath me and the leaching cold of the stone under my feet. We would laugh together at the busy scuttle of people – those who knew the square angling their umbrellas just as the wind catches the water of the fountains and the tourists getting a sudden soak. I sat there until the rain started up again in earnest and then stumbled the cold out of my bones with a walk to the Northern Quarter and towards our bar.

The sex shop you always peer in at – don't pretend you don't – has boards nailed up over its window. Someone more curious, or less open-minded, than you must have put the glass through. The red light still pulses between the planks. Still open for business. I thought of calling in and picking you up something. But really, Alice, the place is ancient. I've never seen anyone come in or out, but I can almost smell the stale spunk and see the shifty eyes of men turn as I enter. I didn't stop. You're worth more than that.

Our bar is busy, but you're not here. I stand in front of the mirror distorted by optics, waiting for the barman to notice me. I peel off my raincoat and rub a hand through my hair, scanning the crowd behind me for your blonde head. I suppose I should be glad you're not here in this lively scrum of laughter and smoke. That you're not enjoying yourself without me. But I never wished my own isolation on you.

I trust you, Alice. I know you love me, just as I love you.

A girl comes and leans on the bar beside me, a five-pound note tilted out of the pinch of her fingers and a painted smile ready for the barman. I'm on my third whisky. I've found a stool and I'm writing to you.

'You a writer?' she asks. The music is loud; I can feel the bass-line through my feet. The girl lays a hand on my arm. Chipped black nail polish; she must bite her nails. 'Hey, lonely man, you writing a book or something?'

'I'm writing to my girlfriend. It's a letter.' I try not to look up. Not to encourage her. Her hand is still on my arm.

'Shame. I had a bet with my friends that I could get into your book.'

She is just a girl. Midlands accent, slurring towards northern. Probably just another student, fresh to the city, desperate for a story to prove she really is having the best years of her life.

(Later)

I drank with them for a while. The girl and her student friends. In fact, I drank too long. I allowed myself to forget about you for a couple of hours. Can you forgive me?

I started as a novelty: the lonely writer man Kelly picked up at the bar. We bought each other drinks and smoked each other's cigarettes. They claimed our bar as a 'find' and questioned me about places to hang out. I told them about my afternoon on the bench and they laughed their public school laughs and called me a weirdo. Kelly wanted a job behind the bar and she had an eye out for the manager. I realised that was who she'd taken me for – a sour note to her flirting. But they were nice kids.

I suppose I drank too much. I sat next to Linda, the smallest and quietest of the group. They were all dressed strangely, but she was wearing an odd calf-length dress which looked as if it was made of paper. I couldn't keep from touching it. 'What is this? It's beautiful.'

'Hey! Hands to yourself, writer boy.' That was one of the lads with them. A big rugby-type called Christian with hair styled so he looked as if he'd run up against a wall. But he was good-natured and smiling.

I laughed up at him, my fingers still folding and unfolding the fabric of Linda's sleeve, suddenly finding skin with a quick pinch. She flinched away from me, but I laid a hand on her arm, just the way Kelly had done to me at the bar. I stroked the soft hairs of her arm as if I were petting an animal and let my fingers play over her black skin, feeling the flesh spring up under my fingers like piano keys. I whispered something to that effect into her tiny ear.

'Seriously mate, let go of her!' Christian again. He pushed his big manly body between me and Linda, and forced me up on to my feet. Big and manly, but not as big as me. To give him credit, he managed to hold his ground. He had enough pints in him to give him courage. Besides, the girls were watching us now, gathered round Linda as if something terrible had happened.

'I think it's time you left.' That was Kelly, stepping in to line with their champion. No trace of the northern twang now. No friendliness either.

'And don't forget this.' Christian tossed the pages of this letter at me. I walked out into the rain. I didn't want to fight children. Somehow found my way back to Aubrey's and it was there I remembered you.

You see what happens when I'm left alone? I need you, Alice. You are the one who keeps me safe.

Forgive me,

Daniel

15th January
Manchester

Dear Mab –

It's always puzzled me that you never wanted to know more about my work with Aubrey. You must think me a kind of glorified secretary. Maybe that is what I am. But us copy-typists are in demand, I'll have you know. Aubrey's lucky to have me. Unfortunately, I have to have him at the same time.

'Let's talk about the paintings for a while.'

'Let's talk about me getting out of this room for a couple of hours. I have things to do, Aubrey.'

'Relax, will you? Oh, go on and smoke if you must.'

'You've got me for five minutes. Why do you want to know about the paintings? We've talked Dad's work to death. Why do you want to bring all that up again?'

'Your sister mentioned some new works. I may have seen some photographs…'

So you told him about them, did you? And you've been sharing pictures? Nice. You and he have such a beautiful relationship, sometimes I'm loath to get in the way.

'Yes, I found some old canvases when I was at the studio. Portraits, would you believe? I bet you've read all there is to read about Dad, so you must know how he felt about portraits.'

'I think "obscene" was the term that stuck in my mind.'

'Yes, well. Always good for a joke, was Dad. And never one to let anyone throw a word at him that he couldn't throw right back.'

'I think we're getting off point here. It was the nature of these portraits that I wished to discuss with you. Or, should I say, the subject matter?'

'Oh, now we're really treading old turf. You really want to go back over that old business? Again? OK. OK. He'd painted me, Sarah, and himself. The self-portraits were the most interesting. I never thought he – '

'When do you think these portraits were painted? Could you tell?'

'I don't know. Probably after he kicked me out. OK, if I'm honest, straight after he kicked me out.'

'And how did they make you feel?'

'Does it ever bother you? Being a walking, talking cliché, I mean? I don't know how they made me feel. They're paintings. You know I can't really ever *see* my father's work the way other people can. It's too close. I can't get it in focus. Maybe I'm just not as willing to lay a load of claptrap on top of it as others seem to be. They fucking love it.'

'But this is the first time he painted you?'

'Yes.'

'Come now, Daniel, you must have had some reaction? Wasn't there anything in the paintings that you responded to? Which triggered memories or emotions.'

'Not really. They're good, I suppose. That's all. It's Dad's work – what's it got to do with me? The subject doesn't paint the picture, does he? Now, you've had your five minutes. Goodbye.'

You see how he tries to get into my head? I have the feeling you encourage him. Please stop.

Daniel

15th January
Manchester

Dear Alice –

I must have missed you again. Ridiculous. I've had so much time for so long and now I'm close to you I can't get my hands on you. Instead, I'm stuck with Aubrey all day and standing at your door in the dark, pushing these letters through your letterbox.

I thought I saw you today in the women I passed. I'm putting you together piece by piece from the faces and bodies of others. What I want is the complete picture. What I want is you, my darling.

Daniel x

18th January
Manchester

Dear Mab –

What have you said to Aubrey now? This is my life, Mab. How dare you try to manipulate my friends? And he is my friend, you know. I've certainly spent more time with him than either you or your mother have. I know I let you down with Dad, I know you think I just ran out on my responsibilities and my promises to you, but I don't deserve this.

I have a girlfriend, whom I love, here. I have a job, which I tolerate, here. I did have a home of sorts, until you started bullying my landlord. Aubrey is so despicably weak when it comes to you. He'll believe anything you tell him. I dread to think what you've been whispering in his ear to have him react the way he did last night.

'Daniel, is that you? Late back, aren't you?'

'I was with my girlfriend.'

'Yes, well. Before you head up, could we have a quick word?'

'I have the notes from today typed up. I'll give you the memory stick tomorrow.'

'No. I mean, it's not a work chat I had in mind. Come and sit a moment. That's it. Now how are things with you?'

'Listen, I'm not really in the mood for another session, Aubrey.'

'Good. That's good. It's just I was speaking to your sister today. She's been having some trouble getting hold of you. And she mentioned your dad isn't doing too well. Something about an infection. Seems he's had to go back into the hospital.'

Is that right, Mab? Is it his leg? Well, you can't go asking me to care. It's nothing to do with me any more.

And then he told me, 'Mab suggested you were needed back. "Now more than ever", I think her words were. All rather dramatic. And, before you start on your usual tirade, I have to say I agree with her. This situation, you living here and working for me, I don't think you've ever really understood… or maybe you have. The point is, Dan, I don't think we can continue. I think the time has come for a move. Your job is always here, of course, but living here in my house now… well, I'm not sure that's the best plan for you at the moment. Not when you're needed elsewhere.'

'You're kicking me out?'

'I wouldn't put it quite like that. It's just, the arrangement between your sister and me requires a certain amount of co-operation, and this is one of those occasions when…'

Arrangement? Mab? You don't even like him.

'I have a great deal of respect for your sister,' he went on. 'For her work and her person. And of course for your whole family. You must admit, you are resistant to all my methods of helping you. You won't talk. You refuse to even contemplate re-establishing a medical regime. Therefore, when Mabel asks me to do something, I must do my best for her.'

'What about doing your best for me? What about your respect for me?'

What on earth do you have on him, Mab? What on earth could have changed so that he's willing to push me out on to the street?

I hope you know what it is you're destroying here. And I hope you know I will kick and fight all the way back to the Studio. I was finding happiness here; why must you ruin that?

Daniel

23rd January
The Studio

Dear Alice –

The only warm room in the house is downstairs with the wood-burner. Dad was never much of a believer in the comforts of central heating. So downstairs we sweat, and upstairs, where I'm hiding, the air is so cold you can watch your breath dissolve into it. I'm under my covers; the sheets are chilled and feel damp against my skin. It must have been like this before I left, but it seems so much colder now I have the memory of your warmth only hours behind me.

Maggie is not talking to me. Dad is, as usual, not talking. Tatty was the only one who seemed delighted at my return. In fact, she is the only one who reacted when I came through the door, unless a grunt from Maggie counts for anything. So much for Mab's promises.

I miss you, my darling. I miss the weight of your shoulder against mine as we lay together with the coloured paper lanterns ticking on their strings as the heat rose from your warm bed. I miss the smell and taste of you. I miss the sweet shudder of your body as I entered you and the soundless gasp of your lips waiting to be smothered by my mouth. I miss my fingers dragging through your electric hair, down the smooth curve of the sea-sucked shell of your pale back. I miss the heft of your thigh. I miss the crooked quality of your smile. There is too much for me to miss all at once, I have to miss you piecemeal. It's the only way I can bear it.

I'm so glad I found you again. And I am so sorry, Alice. I'm sorry I've ever had to leave you, but to do it twice… I still can't quite believe I'm back here. Curled up in bed, in this ill-lit room, wearing all the clothes I left Manchester in, including my coat, with a hard-on. I am ridiculous without you.

At least this time it is finite. Mab promises it won't be long, my darling, and I'll be back with you. That is the one promise Mab must keep. I'm sure she can even talk Aubrey round to our way of thinking. She'll make sure he'll take me back again. She owes me.

Forgive me and don't forget to miss me.

Your Daniel xx

25th January
The Studio

Dear Mab –

Things continue to be frosty – in all senses of the word. The routine has slipped back into place with terrifying ease and I have taken my role in it: dog-walker; bed-changer; arse-washer; waiter; chef; collector of piss and shit and blood and any other fluid that dog or man wishes to throw at me.

Maggie has progressed the silent treatment into a series of barked orders, which she tosses my way at the most unexpected moments; last time was through the toilet door, just as I'd settled down with the paper. I am expected to carry out these orders immediately and without complaint. This is the only way to win back her approval and assistance. This I learnt by dawdling on the toilet – she left the bag of dirty washing behind and only made Dad a cup of tea before she left.

Talk to her for me, could you?

Daniel

28th January
The Studio

Dear Aubrey –

I may not be speaking to you after you kicked me unceremoniously into the gutter, but that doesn't mean I can't write to you about a conversation I had with someone else.

I was pottering around the living room, searching for the emergency tobacco. Dad was watching TV and Maggie was in the kitchen redoing the washing-up I'd finished before she arrived.

'Maggie? Are these yours?'

'You'll have to come through. I can't clean and see through walls.'

I carried the bottles of nail varnish to the kitchen. 'I found them on the bookshelves. You been dolling yourself up?'

'Hardly my colour, are they? That one there looks no better than this dishwater.' Maggie snapped a tea-towel from the rail and wiped the suds from her forearms. She nodded at the bottles in my hand. 'They'll be Sarah's. Give them here, lad. I'll get them back to her.'

'When was Sarah here?'

'What did you expect? Someone had to look after Michael while you were off gallivanting. What did you think, that I was doing it all on my lonesome? That girl was a godsend. She'd give up anything for Michael. Do anything to keep him happy.' She swiped the inside of a coffee cup with the tea-towel. 'Did no one ever teach you how to wash dishes? You use too much liquid and not enough elbow grease. This lot were a right state.'

'Is she coming back?'

'That's what we were wondering about you. Disappearing in the middle of the night and then phoning me up whimpering like a child. Leaving your father high and dry in that god-awful place. Who did you think it was that fetched the doctor and got your dad to the hospital when he was raving? Half out of his mind, he was, poor man. And where were you when you were needed?'

'I know, I know. But Maggie, what about Sarah?'

'What about her?' Maggie laid a final saucer into the stack and twisted her hip to settle against the draining board. 'Don't start all that business again, Danny. It's not right and you know it. Forcing a poor girl out of the only home she'd ever known. Now hand over that nail polish.'

I didn't. I pocketed them. I took the chair next to the bookshelf and sat there imagining her painting her nails Nose Bleed, Corpse Pallor and Yellow Snow. I wondered what the colours said about her mood. She must have stayed here. Maybe she slept in my bed again.

I used to paint her nails for her, back when she first arrived and we were making friends. I was quite the accomplished manicurist: one stroke to the centre; one stroke either side. Apparently it helps to lengthen the nail. *Don't colour over the lines, Danny.* She never wore make-up in the time I knew her and she bit those nails of hers down to the quick, but she liked to have the ragged ends painted over in bright glossy colours.

Her favourite colour back then was gold. I used to watch, magpie-like, her nails' glittering dance in the light of the kitchen as she talked and flirted with Dad in the evenings. I liked to repair the cracks and chips in the paint after a hard day's work in the pond, her finger-pads still crinkled from the water. The polish would slide over the gaps, but it was impossible to make them smooth again. The wounds still showed, scarred dips puckering the smooth surface.

Maggie was foolish to worry about my heart. That is safely stowed with Alice. There is nothing to fear in that regard. The main thing is, Sarah came back, and I must find a way of making her come again.

There are the paintings, of course. They are still gathering dust up in the studio. I don't even know if Sarah has seen them yet. Still, something about them makes me want her never to see them. After all, this time, I only have to put things right. Not make things worse.

Daniel

30th January
The Studio

Dear Mab –

I wonder, sometimes, how much of my life is scripted by you, Mab.

Since your letter, I've been considering Dad's portraits more seriously. I have followed instructions, you needn't worry: I contacted Dad's agency in London and told them about the new work. They were predictably thrilled, even though I made clear the state of the canvases. Portraits are big business, it seems. Even bigger business than naked girls. I suppose there is a certain type of rich person who prefers to have a stranger's face on their wall, rather than a stranger's arse. And that type of rich person likes to buy. I may have shared this choice wisdom with the agency; all I got in response was some drivel about the lurking sexual drives in all the Laird work. They haven't even sniffed the oil paint and already they're harking on about hidden depths!

It was quite fun talking to the agency. I'd forgotten – as you never do – just how much we can trade on the Laird name to behave however we want. As if the eccentricity of artists is hereditary. I insisted on talking to a man in the end – all the well-meaning, earnest girls with degrees were getting on my nerves – and I have to say he was charming. Peter assured me of their full co-operation and discretion and insisted on detailing the long history of services they had provided to Dad and his eminent peers. I could tell he was excited.

Then I found this piece in the paper this morning.

Laird Portraits Discovered

Rumours abound concerning a cache of new portraits found at the home of artist Michael Laird (1937–).

Laird, most famous for his Submerged Nude series (completed 1996), notoriously removed the heads of his subjects when committing them to canvas, claiming 'it is in the sinew and flesh of the body, not of the face, where the true vulnerability of the human condition is expressed'.

The notoriously private artist has received criticism from feminist groups for his 'floating corpses'. However, this present discovery coincides with a resurgence in the popularity of Laird's work. Submerged Nude #6 sold for an undisclosed sum to a private buyer last month. A family source insists this is not an attempt to 'cash in' on an apparently buoyant market, but rather a chance to reflect upon Laird's change of artistic direction in the years following his mysterious departure from public life.

No examples have yet been released for examination, but the art world is buzzing with speculation about the possibility of a new collection. Clement Jones, curator of the National Gallery, stated:

'Michael Laird is one of our greatest living artists. Any new work should, therefore, be eagerly anticipated by both the public and the nation.'

So, national treasure or passing fad? Either way, the expectation is high for a private showing later this year.

I've been fielding calls all day. One idiot, who has managed to purchase one of the Submerged Nude series, requested a portrait of the model in question. 'To match'. He burbled on about 'completing the picture at last'. Money was no object, apparently. It took me an hour to get rid of him.

I've spoken to everyone from serious collectors to tabloid journalists about the 'exciting new discovery at Laird's country home'. They make it sound as if the butler has to call me from the west wing to the telephone, rather than Maggie giving a shout out of the kitchen window to the woodshed. I've been bundled up in Dad's big winter coat all morning, trying to gather kindling. I must call charming Peter and complain about the professed discretion of the agency. I'll be sure to lay the blame firmly at the feet of the graduate girls. It's best to keep at least one of them on side.

This sudden publicity is rather unsettling. I have been careful to avoid any real mention of the subject of the portraits. Well, I've been careful not to mention my own name. Peter was practically drooling at the mention of self-portraits, and that was before I told him Sarah was in evidence. Maybe it's not the publicity, maybe it's the portraits themselves that are getting to me. Peter had me up there straight away, taking as many photographs as possible from different angles and in different lights. I've been spending too much time staring into the faces of my past.

It continues to be ferociously cold. The fire has become the focus of all of our days. Even Dad has been moved back towards it and away from the TV without complaint. I can't seem to keep him warm. I suppose it's that he's so inactive sitting in his chair all day, with only the short stagger to bed in the evening getting him moving at all. But I don't dare take him out. The ice is thin, but deadly slippery. Our neighbour kindly shovelled some building sand along our section of pavement. Maggie took him out a mug of tea and a slice of her special fruit cake, left over from Christmas. I steered clear of it. I think there may be romance in the air, and, besides, I didn't fancy being forced to lend a hand.

I'm to parcel up the paintings as best I can and get them to the agents. More instructions to follow! Meanwhile, write, or phone – if you can get through – and tell me what I should be saying. I know it could make us some serious money, selling these pictures. I know we could set Dad up in style in a nursing home and I could escape back to my Alice. Just tell me it's a good idea.

Daniel

30th January
The Studio

Dear Freya –

Happy New Year! And thank you so much for your letters. I've been a little distracted since Christmas – I'm sure you've heard all your mother's complaints! But I'm back now, and catching up on my correspondence with you was one of the few pleasures waiting for me on my return. The painting you sent is fantastic (and I call it a painting, because there is no way you should discredit it with the term 'doodle'). You've managed to catch Tatty perfectly – I especially liked the wings! I showed it to your grandad and he held on to it for a long time. I think that's his way of showing real appreciation.

Paintings have been much the theme around here. It seems your grandad is to have another exhibition. It also seems that I'm going to be the one to organise it. I must have seriously upset your mother! I've hung your offering up in the kitchen. I think it looks perfect there. Maybe I'm more qualified for this job than I realised?

Tell your mother to bring you across for the exhibition when it happens. It would be wonderful to meet you again and I know a little rag-tag dog who would smother you in kisses.

Do write again soon,

Uncle Dan

30th January
The Studio

Dear Alice –

A week away from you is a week too long. Remind me what you feel like and how you smell.

How I wish I had more photographs of you, although our session in front of the camera has been a great comfort to me. I took the film to a place on the market to be developed – well, I could hardly have taken those shots to Boots! Anyway, I didn't know the man on the stall. You needn't worry about my embarrassing you. He didn't even wink as he handed over the prints. I was rather disappointed.

My favourite is the one we took where you are falling away from me, your body stretched out in abandoned pleasure and your hands above your head. Oh, to run a hand up that body, graze my fingers over your neat mound of hair and up to the beautiful swell of your breasts. To take your nipple between my lips and feel it harden against my tongue, the way the models' did in the cold workroom. To hear your cry as you arch against me. I want to push my hands into this photograph and lift you out, my slippery fish, and lay you down beside me. My catch of the day. Then I could truly examine that look on your face, the pleasure and the pain of it, and taste those tears that roll down your face.

Your ever-loving,
Daniel xx

2nd February
The Studio

Dear Alice –

It seems there is to be a party. Well, I'm paraphrasing, but the party appears to be the most important aspect of the upcoming show, according to the calls I've been taking today.

Despite my protests, with help from Dad's agent in London it seems that Dad is to have another exhibition. I had hopes of a quiet sale of some paintings I found. But, though I think Dad's agency had presumed he was long dead, they are certainly keen not to miss out on a show. It seems Dad has got quite famous in his absence. A guy called Peter (whom I'm a little in love with) kept talking about 'encouraging sales statistics' and the way Dad's 'artistic direction tapped right into the vein of modern ennui'. Remarkable, especially when you consider most of his work was completed nine years ago and at the present moment Dad couldn't tell his ennui from his elbow.

Peter was disappointed not to be able to talk to Dad directly about the paintings in question. I've played down the extent of his illness, managing to make multiple strokes sound like an eccentric life choice. I don't want anything to mess up these sales. If we can make enough then we could get Dad into some kind of full-time care and then he'd be safe and looked after and I could come back to you. It's not long to wait, is it?

You should come. To the party and the exhibition. You do look so beautiful in art galleries. You could wear that blue dress of yours, the one you try to play down with biker boots and heavy jackets. I'll buy you a pair of heels and you can be my personal flapper. I know you have to work, but surely you could take a couple of days and come down? Just this once. Then I can show you off to everyone. I'm sure Mab thinks you're a figment of my imagination. I'll get the agency to send you a proper invitation when they're printed. I'm busy co-ordinating this end of the whole thing from Dad's old writing desk. Impressive, aren't I? Promise you'll think about it, when you're not thinking of me.

Daniel xx

4th February
The Studio

Dear Aubrey –

I'm running an office. This is no exaggeration. I am the full-time carer and now, apparently, the full-time personal assistant of the great Michael Laird. Someone actually asked for me by that title. It's worse than working for you; at least then I got paid for my trouble. Still, hopefully there will be plenty of money to come! It's strange, but preparations for the exhibition appear to be continuing without my interference or agreement. I don't know why they keep phoning; they all seem to know far more about what's going on than me.

With at least some concession to the state of Dad, they are going to have the first show up here, in the old workhouse on the outskirts of town. I think the agency likes the idea of wheeling Dad out and showing him off alongside the paintings, and, as I refused to attempt the trip to London with him, we needed a local venue. So London is coming to us. Most people are phoning to bitch about having to travel – you'd think the world ended at Liverpool Street station.

I used to play at the workhouse when I was a kid. There were always stories about it being haunted. Me and a couple of my friends got dragged up there by Mab one summer. The summer she got her first camera. She took photos of the derelict rooms and abandoned furniture and terrified us with whispers of 'Did you hear that?' All I heard was mice (the suspicion of rats was enough to frighten me) and our own footsteps on the old boards, but Mab claimed to hear the singing of children, the rocking of an old chair and a mysterious weeping on the stairs. She was always good for a story. She got one of my friends, Neil Coleman, so wound up that his mother came round to the studio to complain about Mab's influence.

I think the workhouse was already being used by the small pottery that leases it today, so we were probably trespassing when we went on our ghost-hunt. Anyhow, they want me to go and talk to the woman at Smashing

Plates and view the space they're making available for us. Dad's agency have organised a curator and I'm to meet her there on Tuesday.

At least it will be a chance to get out of the house. Dad's been pretty difficult recently. I suppose I've got used to the problems we've had – the incontinence, the lack of speech, the lack of mobility, the drinking and the occasional fall – but lately it's been hard to even keep him in his chair. And he keeps howling, like a dog in pain. It scares the life out of Tatty. If it carries on, I'll have to get the doctor in. It'll be no good bringing him to the exhibition if all he tries to do is bite the buyers.

And, before you ask, you're not invited to the show.

Daniel

6th February
The Studio

Dear Mab –

Dad's bad. They say the urine infection he had when I left has come back. It's bloody awful. It's as though he's gone mad.

At first I thought the part of his mind I'd hoped was gone forever in one of those little explosions in his brain – the part that hates me – had connected back up: that those dangling synapses had finally joined hands and made a fist. He charged at me in the morning when I came downstairs to wake him. He hadn't got his teeth in, but his cheeks were taut, his hands clawing at my shirt and arms. He

111

was bellowing and crying something which sounded a lot like 'Sarah'. It took a while for me to realise he was staring right through me, towards the door. Thank God I'd locked up. Who knows how long he'd been wandering. Tatty was under the table, hiding, silent and terrified.

The doctor has dosed him up on antibiotics, but has warned they could take a while to kick in. He said a little mild confusion was normal and I shouldn't let it worry me. I'm beginning to hate that doctor.

It means it may be difficult to get away and meet the curator at the workhouse. I may have to get her to reschedule? Or she could just come here and look at the paintings? I can direct her up the road. There's no real need for me to go, anyway; I know what the workhouse looks like.

Some of the canvases are still in need of attention. I shipped off the best of them, but dreamboat Peter keeps calling and asking for more for the catalogue. Apparently, the unfinished work will help create a story of Dad's decline. I think they'd be happier if he were just dead and buried; then they'd know how to play it. It will be interesting to see what they'll do if he's in the same state for the exhibition. If they don't seem sure how to market a living corpse, I wonder what they'll do with a raving one.

(Later)

Sarah came. She is still here. Maggie must have told her Dad was sick.

I know it must be hard for her to see Dad and me together in the same room, but she didn't have to react like that when I walked through from the kitchen. She didn't even say hello, just started and froze. Saying that, I nearly poured Dad's dinner over myself when I saw her, so I guess we were both nervous. She hurried over to Dad's chair and squatted down beside him on the side closest to the wall. You would have thought I was threatening to pour the dinner down *her*. Maggie hustled me over to my chair by the fire and she and Sarah helped Dad with his meal.

It is quite peaceful sitting here, listening to the two women talk and fuss over Dad. He's actually quite capable of feeding himself, but they seem to enjoy cutting up his food and spooning it to his mouth. He is indifferent to them, busy watching the television and laughing along every time the canned stuff is cued. The girls have to time their feeding carefully, but he's already covered in half-chewed mashed potato and beans.

Sarah looks lovely – what I can see of her. Her face is turned up into the warm light from the TV, chasing and flashing shadow across her features. She looks younger tonight, almost the Sarah I remember. You needn't worry about me, Mab. This is an exercise of nostalgia; the beauty I see in her now is her resemblance to Alice. You know I've only really ever been able to focus on one woman at a time. And I don't intend to get hurt like that again.

I should invite Sarah to the exhibition, though, don't you think? Most of the portraits are of her, after all. Peter would love it: the Laird Muse in the flesh. He'll probably dig their own pond and have her floating in it among the canapés.

Oh, dear, Dad has just flipped the dinner plate and tried to put his hands up Maggie's dress. I guess peace was too much to hope for. I'd better go and help.

Love to Freya,

Daniel

6th February
The Studio

Dear Aubrey –

Sarah just left. You would have been proud of me. I was the very definition of self-control. She looked amazing. She was dressed in some kind of blue slinky thing with shadows that hinted at the flesh moving below. It was nice that she dressed up for me, but it was also confusing. I had just begun to adjust myself to the idea that all that business with her was in the past.

It took me no time at all to fall in love with Sarah, but for her, I believe, it was a gradual process. She had to learn to trust me. I was the one who waited for her at the end of a long day working. I was the one who dried her tears when Dad grew furious with a painting and threatened to give her up. I'd learnt from the other girls that an artist often blamed the model if a piece of work went badly. I was the one who taught her how to please him, passing on the tricks the other models talked about. If I thought she was aware of my feelings for her, I presumed she'd just take me for a chubby teenager with a crush, but I underestimated the value of our evenings together. There is nothing like a shared history.

One evening, Dad was in a rage about the composition of a new piece. He'd been in a rage all week. Sarah was ill, suffering from vertigo. She'd been to the doctor's and been given a strip of tiny white pills, but they didn't seem to have any effect. She said that, even secure in the pool, she was terrified of falling. She said she knew it was ridiculous but her blood wouldn't believe her. It swam around her head, tilting her off balance, and popped and danced in her limbs.

She panicked and wept and couldn't keep still. At first, Dad attempted sympathy. He let the underground pipes warm the pool for over an hour before she got in to pose; he fed her red meat and dark chocolate and swapped her morning coffee for fresh fruit juice. When she broke pose he massaged her legs and rubbed her temples with soft gliding strokes. They both gave up cigarettes on an empty stomach. Nothing helped. Finally, he lost his temper.

Sarah came in shaking with cold and misery. Dad said he'd eat at the pub and told me not to wait up. He said nothing to Sarah. I listened as she wept, and lit the fire, though the evening was warm and Dad hated us to waste wood. Then I went into the kitchen to pour Sarah a drink.

Earlier that day, on my way back from my last GCSE exam, I'd walked to the shop under the footbridge. I'd taken off my tie and school jumper and stuffed them into my backpack with my books. With my top buttons undone and my hair swept back, I had hoped to pass myself off as an office worker. As an adult. If I'd bothered to glance at my reflection in the glass door on my way in I would have seen that all I'd done was expose my spotty forehead and dirty collar.

There was a new girl behind the counter. She looked young. She must have been older than she looked, because she smiled when I walked in. Girls my own age didn't smile at me. There were smudges of glitter at the corner of her eyes and a ring through her bottom lip.

'It's Daniel, isn't it?' she asked. 'I used to go to school with your sister.'

I didn't remember her, but for some reason I felt ashamed as I passed over my pack of sausages and my oven chips.

'A friend of mine's sick,' I explained. 'I'm looking after her.'

She nodded. She probably wasn't much interested. I'd lost the smile.

'You've given me too much here.' She handed me back the second twenty-pound note, one of the two I'd slipped from Dad's wallet that morning. 'You're lucky I'm honest.'

'Actually, I'll take a bottle of that brandy behind you.'

The girl was smiling again. Her lip ring bounced up to tickle her cupid's bow. I wondered how anyone kissed her. She took a quick look around the shop. There were no other customers.

'It'll be good for your sick friend. My mum swears by it, says there's nothing a nip won't cure. Never had much of a taste for the stuff myself. Me and your sister always went for vodka. You should try that. Just mix it with a bit of lime cordial. Knocks you right off your feet and it's half the price of this stuff. No? Well, it's your money.'

She packed the brandy into a carrier bag, wedging the oven chips and sausages around it. She winked. 'You have a good night, Daniel. Do something I wouldn't.'

Behind the ring and the glitter, her face was childlike, her eyes a vacant blue. I wondered if Mab would remember her.

That was the night it all happened. I didn't expect it.

Sarah's laughter when I brought through the tumblers of brandy: *You've used the wrong glasses, Danny*. Our whispered talk in front of the fire. Her tearstained face suffused in the flush of alcohol. My voice announcing that we should make a commitment to drink down to the belly of the bottle. My voice announcing toasts: *To Your Health! Bottoms Up! Up Yours!* It was the first time I'd ever been drunk. Laughter, so much laughter – not all of it can have been my own.

The fire dying and our stumbled walk up the stairs to the workroom. My hand reaching out to brush her behind as it swayed in front of me.

Play, it was all play. The thrill of the chase, isn't that what they call it? The lover's tussle: a mess of hands and nails and arms and fists. Sarah on the floorboards with masking tape in her hair. The surprising weight of her naked breast in my hand. My shirt torn. Peeling the band of my underpants over my erection with one hand, while the other explored her flesh laid open before me.

She was saying something, but her features were foggy; her voice a background whine. I was absorbed in the delicious urgency of it all. Her mouth open. I leant to kiss her silent. Her eyes closed. Why is she crying? Why, with so much pleasure, could she be crying?

And then there was Dad. Back early from the pub and ready to ruin everything.

(Later)

I upset myself, running back over the past. Why are you always preaching about it being so 'useful'? I was so desperate I even tried another exercise of yours suggested for such situations. You can imagine how galling it is to eventually find perspective through your advice. Here are the results.

Ten things I remember about Sarah:

1. She liked her tea stewed to the colour of a chicken's egg. Brown, not white.

2. Her lips were always dry. She would gnaw on them until they were raw and then paste them over with balm. Her mouth tasted sweet and smelt of strawberries.

3. When she posed for Dad, she would always turn her eyes to the right. The direction liars look when asked a question.

4. She liked to make faces into the bathroom mirror and watch for my reaction over her shoulder.

5. She held a pen as if it were trying to escape from her. When she wrote, she pushed so hard into the paper that it curled.

6. When she could afford it, she smoked vanilla tobacco in liquorice papers. She called it her 'little luxury'. Dad hated them. He said they made her taste like burnt custard.

7. We had a favourite joke, which both of us forgot. The punch line was 'them's the breaks'. She and I would just have to say 'them's the breaks' to each other if we wanted the other to laugh.

8. When she read *The End of the Affair*, she cried for a full hour just because Henry knew.

9. She often told me she loved me.

10. She didn't try to stop him.

Daniel

12th February
The Studio

Dear Mab –

Clarissa Morrison arrived today from the agency. All spiky shoes, big hair and lipstick. She asked me to call her something that sounded like 'Claggy', so I avoided calling her anything. What happened to dreamboat Peter – why couldn't he have come? And whatever happened to the dusty old chap who used to come for Dad's paintings? I don't ever remember him speaking. I don't actually remember a moment with this one when she wasn't saying something.

'Ah, you must be the son. Daniel or Danny? Do you mind if I call you Danny? Things go so much easier if one keeps it informal, don't you find? Had a devil of a time finding you. And here's my card. Now none of that Clariss-a business, I'm [indecipherable 'Claggy' word]. Now let me in, there's a darling. I'm simply dying to see the place where the magic happens. I'm a massive Laird fan and I mean MASSIVE. Never had the pleasure… oh, is that Mr Laird himself? I wasn't prepared. Do I look all right? I can't believe I'll actually get to… Didn't have much time with my hair, what with the drive and everything. I'll just wander over and introduce myself, shall I?

'Michael, can I call you Mike? I'm [indecipherable], from the agency, we're *really* excited about the show and I mean REALLY. I'd be privileged if you could spare a couple of moments to chat. Just see if we can't get a couple of novel quotes for the programme. Oh, I seem to have upset him. I see – in the way of the telly, am I? Well, we all like our favourite shows; wouldn't like to miss them.

'Danny, darling, is there anything that we can do for Mike to kind of... spruce him up a little for the show? I mean, don't get me wrong, I know these artists can be eccentric and all that, but we're in a competitive market here. Hateful phrase, but there you are. We're dragging people up from London and there are expectations to be met, Danny. If it's a question of financing, then... Ah, really, no speech at all? We were rather hoping for a short talk of some kind. A little introduction, if you will. No? Well, not to worry, that's why I'm here. We'll find some workaround, I'm sure.

'Now, these paintings, may I have a quick look-see? Oh, what a quaint little staircase. Quite a tight squeeze, but nothing I can't handle.

'Ah, I see. Yes, the canvases really are in a state. No, please don't even try to separate them. Leave them as they are and we'll pack them into the car. Get them straight to the experts and let them sort it out. That's the way, Danny. Can you take one more? Perfect. Yes, well, I'm afraid I have what's termed a delicate back. Have to rely on big strong boys like you. Let's get these to the car. I'm parked just outside. Then we can get over to this wonderful space you've found. Oh, really? Well, surely he'll be fine left alone for a few hours? Mike? [Cue painfully loud and slow voice reserved for addressing of idiots and small children.] I was just saying to Danny here, you'll be fine on your own.

'My goodness, what a noise! You horrible little dog, get off! Whatever is the matter? Am I in front of the television again? Really, I mean, is this normal? Danny, darling, do make it stop.'

I was really quite proud of Dad, but, despite his hollering, I was bullied into accompanying Claggy to the workhouse. The woman from Smashing Plates was waiting for us, dressed in the uniform washed-out denim and floral patterns of the ageing hippy artist. Karen Appleby. Apparently I went to school with her son. Claggy barely acknowledged her.

We were shown into a large room on the first floor of the workhouse. Original windows let the afternoon light pour over raw red brick walls and fresh-stripped floorboards, which ached under our feet. There was an old potter's wheel in one corner along with piles of dust sheets and a collection of cleaning supplies. The smell of dry clay dust and worked wood.

'We took down the dividing walls last summer,' Karen explained, cranking one of the windows open. 'Thought it might make a good workroom or display room. But to be honest the space kind of got away from us. We have all we need downstairs. This building is quite a responsibility. It takes most of our effort keeping the kids out. Vandalism and that.'

I managed not to blush, wondering if my initials are still alongside yours, carved in the stairway on the far side of the building. Claggy was in raptures about the light, which seemed pointless to me considering Dad's exhibition is at night. She sniffed around the dust sheets and felt the walls, talking all the while about 'progression of images' and 'ideal locations'. Finally she turned on Karen with questions about parking, reception rooms and 'ambience controls' (which I eventually translated as the removal of all evidence of Smashing Plates' trade before the show began). There was no need for me to be there. In the end – or should I say when I realised there was no end in sight – I made my excuses and walked back to the studio. I don't think Claggy even noticed me leave, but the Smashing Plates woman looked close to tears.

Dad was fine. Still watching the TV roll ever onwards with Tatty at his feet.

Love to Freya and to you,

Daniel

12th February
The Studio

Dear Freya –

I hope I haven't written anything to offend you. Maybe you are just busy with all your friends and schoolwork? I hope so. I would be grateful if you could spare the time to put pen to paper and tell us all about it. I make sure to read your letters aloud – when we get them – so Grandad and Tatty can hear your news. Tatty is a wonderful listener. She sits up with her back straight and perks up her ears. Well, I should say 'ear'. One of her ears must have been through a bit of a battle, because it doesn't stand up like the other one. Her past is a bit of a mystery. Just like your present.

Do write soon,

Uncle Dan

16th February
The Studio

Dear Alice –

I'm writing this letter in the bath. This is not as complicated as it sounds: Dad has one of those bath-tidy things made of wood. I have a bottle of cold beer propped up next to these pages. It's all very cosy. So you don't need to worry that this letter is marked by lonely tears; it's just me being careless with the bathwater. Well, mostly that.

It seems unnatural to keep my hands out of the water. I can feel my body pumping the heat through my blood up into my wrists. I can almost see them steaming. I like a hot bath. I like the water. I can rarely wait until the tub's full before lowering myself in. I like to squat, with my hands and feet submerged and my arse pulled up to keep my genitals out of the water. I let them steam a little before I introduce them to the heat. Once my cock and balls are in, I'm in. I throw my head back and under and listen to the water from the taps thrum against the bottom of the bath. The only sound in my own world. No TV noise; none of Dad's weird complaining keens; no Maggie, barking orders; nothing but my thoughts of you.

How I'd love to take a bath with you. To introduce you to the hot water, piece by piece. There would need to be bubbles and perfumed liquids to pour under the running taps, the scent lifting up to mingle with your own. Candles too, with their private, finite flicker, gathering us closer to each other. A licking light, in which I would wash you gently, as you stood before me, calf-deep in the water. I'd rub the bubbles up your body, up your flanks, my face so close I could feel the bubbles break under my breath, hear their crackle as they stretched over your skin and slid back towards the water. I'd ease you down between my knees and soap your wild hair, snatching kisses from your upturned lips as I brush the suds away from your closed eyes.

Or maybe I'd just like to watch you bathe. Watch you, without you knowing you are watched. So that you are perfectly natural. I wonder how you get into the bath; how you strip off your own clothes when you're alone, without my eager eyes upon you; what you do in that private world behind the bathroom door. My only private place of late. My own private view and there's only one invitation. To you. Accept this, my darling, please. I need you here.

Missing you always,

Your Daniel

21st February
The Studio

Dear Aubrey –

I had a letter from Mab. She's arranged for one of the theatre companies she makes masks for to do some kind of a performance the night before the exhibition. So, I guess she's coming. It's turning into quite the family affair. Maybe I should do card tricks or juggle oranges in the corner?

Apparently the dreadful woman from the agency talked her into getting involved. You can see their reasoning, I suppose. Masks and portraits, it's all about faces after all. The London élite get to make a weekend rather than a night of it and they get two Lairds for the price of one. But I'm surprised at Mab. I never thought she'd hold her own work up against Dad's. She's always claimed they have nothing in common. Perhaps she hopes to outshine him. Or maybe she just needs the money more than I thought. Even more than me.

I don't really understand your pressing me now about getting back on to the medication. This will be simple. I will soon be free. The last thing I need at the moment is my head clouded by prescription drugs.

By the way, you're not invited to this either.

Daniel

1st March
The Studio

Dear Alice –

A sticky type of dream last night, the kind you can't stamp out of your mind for the rest of the day. I was running after you, chasing your beautiful hair through a city which looked like Manchester, but which felt like home.

It started at the bus stops in Piccadilly Gardens. I was trying to get off a bus; a mess of raincoats, wet plastic shoulders and hooded heads obstructed me. Then there were your golden curls, just out of reach. You were wearing your green coat; I could see the collar and your white hand reaching up to adjust it, as the doors of the bus folded shut behind you and I was left sitting next to an old man on those sideways seats that face the stairs. The ones reserved for vulnerable passengers. The ones you are ordered to give up to the pregnant and the old and those with screaming children in tow. I could feel the frayed fabric of the bus seat under my hands. The old man was keening, *It hurts, it hurts.* Over and over, he kept repeating it. And I could not turn and look out through the steamed-up window. I knew I was leaving you, but I couldn't move. It hurts.

Then there was a street, with shops lining either side, and a busy Saturday crowd milling down its length. A bit like Market Street, but not that exactly. Conversations, none aimed in my direction, passed around and over me, a blur of voices and noise, as I was forced along by the stream of clacking feet. Above us was the shadow of a footbridge, a white figure and a little boy. It didn't belong there. There was someone with me – Mab? – an angry silence at my shoulder. I wanted to turn and face them and cling to their feet and weep, but the crowd was pressing me forward.

And then suddenly I saw you. You swung out of a shop, that same green coat, those same blonde locks among the dark, bowed, anonymous heads. The sight of you cast a rope across that crowd, a bright cord of attention, along which I drew myself, threw myself, towards you. I could see the thin stretch of your green back, your neat calves working, the patterns of wear on the soles of your shoes as they flipped up behind you; but I could get no closer. The angry presence at my shoulder had become a weight. It had company. It was a great weight that pinned my feet and made me struggle as if mired in some horrible ooze. I had no voice to scream.

You turned down a side street and I fell after you. For a moment, the scent of your hair. Red bricks and cement, the tail of a cello's song falling from an upper window, your hair luminous in the gloom. But still your back, forever your back to me. There are bags in your hands, your fists gripped around their plastic handles, your painted nails bitten to the quick. A doorway I don't recognise. Another door closing behind you. The image of you, a double-exposure on cheap paintwork. Lost. It hurts.

When I came downstairs, Dad had somehow got the record player working: Schubert's *Death and the Maiden*, String Quartet No.14 in D Minor. I copied that down from the sleeve. I don't know anything about music. I didn't think Dad did either. He's been playing it endlessly, flipping the needle back to the start each time the record plays out. He goes into fits if I venture anywhere near the player.

So we both sit and glower at the fire and I chase you through my dream again and again to the sound of mounting fiddles. I'm sure it's changed my memory of the dream – nothing like a soundtrack to colour the imagination.

It's enough to make me miss the TV.

But, just in case, show your face, my darling.

Daniel

8th March
The Studio

Dear Mab –

It's an odd time. We are all waiting for the exhibition to happen and the days have lost their definition. Nothing exists other than this countdown to noise and people and paintings. The phone keeps ringing with questions I can't answer and problems I don't understand. This doesn't seem to concern the callers; they're just grateful that someone picks up the phone, that they have someone to talk to. One woman actually cried as she told me about her dog dying the week before. I felt like Aubrey, dishing out comfort and advice. London must be a very lonely place.

Dad is back to his normal self after the infection. I am still surprised by how comfortable I am with him. All that worry the doctors gave me about synapses healing and reconnecting, and he is as docile as a well-loved pet. More docile, if compared to Tatty. It feels like a forgiveness of a sort, to be wiped out of his brain like that. A simple series of strokes and I find a new father. I even find myself wishing he could talk.

So far, I've more or less ignored the speech therapist's advice about picture charts or the possibility of electronic gizmos to help him communicate. Well, if I'm truthful, I completely ignored it. I let her come along with the district nurse and play her playschool games with him. If she ever asked, I gave my dutiful face and told them we'd been practising. She must be so disappointed by his progress.

I haven't been treating Dad badly as such. I've just been scared about what might come out of his mouth if he were able to shape words, or point at the right pictures on a card. I guess I'm still a little scared about what might be lurking behind the silence. I imagine it would be something like using a Ouija, placing his hand over the picture board. That same half-terror that he might actually spell out sense.

He gave me a look this morning as I was washing him in the bath. It was tender, Mab, can you imagine that? And it's not just that – there have been a series of such moments since he's recovered from the last illness. When I've woken him up from a night's sleep, he's seemed pleased to see me. Even smiled. And yesterday, when I sat rolling him cigarettes, he came over and took hold of my arm. We stayed like that together for a long time.

Love to Freya and to you,

Daniel

8th March
The Studio

Dear Freya –

I wonder if spring is as nice where you are? I went for a walk with Tatty today. Everything is green and waking up after sleeping through the long cold winter. The field which had been carved into great waves of earth is flat and sprouting. There were even a few little flowers. Tatty watered them.

Still no letter from you. I do miss the sight of one. And didn't you promise me some photographs? It would be nice to see what shape your smiling face has grown into. And then I'll be able to recognise you when you arrive.

Did you get your invitation to the exhibition? It seems your mum is going to give us a bit of a show too. The actors have been booked, she tells me. I suppose it will give the guests something to do the night before the exhibition. Most people are coming for the weekend. You don't need to worry about places filling up; you'll stay here with us. I'll even let you have my room. Tatty can't wait to meet you.

With love,

Uncle Dan

13th March
The Studio

Dear Mab –

I have seen the details of your mask demonstration. I have invited Alice, and am hopeful she will be able to get the time off work. You'll get to meet her at last. Be kind to her, Mab.

I've been letting myself worry about the Alice situation recently. I don't know why, but I feel as if there is something wrong. She is so wonderful; I don't want to lose her. But there is more distance between us than the literal one. I worry that there might be someone else. Last time I was in the bookshop where she works, last time I was in Manchester, there was a guy behind the counter. I didn't recognise him. He must have been new. Alice wasn't there – I think I told you, it took me a while to track her down – but for some reason I could see how they'd be together. He wasn't flashy or anything, he wasn't even particularly good-looking, but there was an easiness about him. They must laugh together, the way I saw him laughing with a customer as he piled up her books next to the till. He looked like the kind of man who touches women as he talks, casually drawing them into an intimacy with a hand on the arm. He hummed as he shelved paperbacks, and that, along with his haircut, made me wonder if he was in a band. He even came over to ask me if I needed any help. I was glad I was taller than him. I was glad there was an angry red rash of spots across the top of his cheeks. But I found myself smiling at him, just because he was smiling at me.

I keep imagining them together. Her smiling back at him, just because he's smiling at her. She wouldn't mean anything by it, she doesn't know how men can be, but she'd like the touches on her arm and the loose friendliness of him. So different from me. She'll tell him about the customers and how they make her cry. Maybe he'll catch her weeping by the bookshelves and just lean in. 'Hey, are you OK?' Then there would be a hug. So natural, that hug. Just a 'Come here, you,' and my girlfriend is in his arms.

She must be lonely without me. Maybe there will be drinks after work. Talk and laughter in our favourite bar. She'll lead him there, keen to show off her find. Keen to impress him. They'll have to bend their heads together to be heard over the music. He'll tell her about his band; maybe invite her to their next gig; share some third-hand anecdotes as if they're his own. He'll pull out all his best lines – she really is that beautiful. And they'll be close, so close. She will have had a couple of drinks and if they found our table then the light would be soft. A kind light for the spotty boy drinking with my girlfriend.

Would she tell him about me? Would she even remember me when she's sitting there with the boy from the bookshop?

Daniel

24th March
The Studio

Dear Aubrey –

I should have known that despite my best efforts you'd manage to get yourself invited. Yes, you can stay here, you cheapskate. Mab – and possibly Freya – will be here too. You might have to bunk up with Dad, but we'll find you a bed.

Sadly, I think I'll actually be pleased to see you. I've been driving myself mad recently. Girl problems. I won't bore you with the details, but I thought that my girlfriend would make it down for the exhibition and it turns out she won't. So, I'm stuck with you as my date. And you're stuck with me. You can't even evict me this time, old boy.

Maybe the show, and all it entails, will be exactly the distraction I need. I'm certainly busy enough. The London types have been on the phone all week, asking me to find reservations for them at one of our finest hotels. The more exacting they sound, the worse the establishment I recommend. They don't seem to mind, though. They are all just crazy about Dad and everything about him. They all want to come to the house and meet him privately. They want to discuss his work and see the pond and generally eye up the fixtures and fittings of our life.

I've put them off as best I can. I don't know what you expect from Dad, but don't expect much. The great artist Michael Laird is at present seated in front of the TV, the lights from some game show reflected on his glasses so vividly it seems to be playing out of his head. The TV is on mute, but he doesn't seem to have noticed. He's naked from the waist down, apart from the catheter snaking from his penis to the bag strapped to his ankle. He did something to the tube this morning and urine leaked all over his trousers. I found him struggling to get himself changed, like a guilty child. I cleaned him up in the bathroom and then sat him on a towel to dry. It didn't seem worthwhile getting him out of the rest of his clothes.

I don't know how we're going to get through next week. I hate to say it, but I think I'm going to need your help, Aubrey.

See you soon,

Daniel

26th March
The Studio

Dear Alice –

No word from you about the exhibition. Are you offended because you didn't get an embossed invitation on thick cream card? The agency sent those out, but they've given me a few for 'family and friends'. I enclose it for you. I need you to come here and be with me.

I'm on my single bed with the duvet thrown over my head, trying to remember the comfort of your sweet smell mingled with my own. Instead, I just breathe my own stink. I realise how petulant and teenage this is, sulking under the duvet. Add a torch and I regress another five years. I should be downstairs. There is the washing-up to do and the catheter bag to empty. Dad tore his hand open somehow yesterday and I have to change his dressing.

I really should get up. I managed to get myself dressed, but thoughts of you, of how far away you are from me, drove me back under the covers with my writing paper. I even have my shoes and socks on. Maggie would complain about the state of the sheets.

Come to me and I'll find us a proper room. Most of the London visitors are staying at the Crown Hotel. A new family have taken it over and spruced it up. The models used to talk about the Crown and the old man who lived in it. His wife had died suddenly long before I was born. It was said that he chased everyone out of the place as soon as he got the news. There were rumours of plates of food half-eaten and board games half-played. A life suspended behind net curtains and dust sheets, with the old man circulating like Miss Havisham at her wedding feast.

I could get us a suite and we could hide away together, rediscover each other, under their sheets. I'll even bring a torch. We could play like children. It would be so innocent and beautiful just to be with you. If you'd only send me a reply and tell me you are coming.

I ask so little of you, Alice, just your fidelity and your affection. I feel as if I'm losing both. Why are you abandoning me when I need you most? I can't understand what I could have done to deserve it. I would never do anything to hurt you or risk our relationship. It's what keeps me sane here. And now I'm losing everything, including that sanity.

I'm desperate, darling. I'm not afraid to say it. Remember that nonsense Aubrey fed you about the river of your thoughts? Well, my river is polluted and full of bloated corpses. I've tried to weigh them down, but they bob to the surface and accuse me with their gaping wounds. You were the one clear stream.

Maybe that's it. Maybe I'm just letting the mess of my rotten life infect you. Or perhaps I smother you? An image comes into my mind. I am walking by a reservoir in the Peak District on a rare day off from Aubrey. Along the line of the water's edge grow trees, or what used to be trees. They are white as bone; their branches claw the dim sky, leafless and bare. The drowned trees, drinking their own demise, a white iris to the eye of the dark lake. Do I drown you? Is this very letter a splash of ink too much?

Tell me what to do, Alice. Tell me how to fix this. Maybe it is time to lay down my pen and run to you again? I could do that, you know. I would do that for you, no matter the consequences. I will always come, Alice. No matter where you are, I will come to you and it will be as it was before.

Yours, always yours,

Your Daniel

INVITATION TO VIEW
THE MOST ANTICIPATED EXHIBITION OF THE DECADE

THE PORTRAITS OF

MICHAEL LAIRD

1st April 2006

7pm
The Workhouse
Upchurch   R.S.V. P.

28th March
The Studio

Dear Alice –

I can't believe you're not here. You're really not going to come, are you? Despite everything I said in my letters, you are going to leave me to go through this alone.

I don't know what I could have said or done differently. I don't understand this silence. And I don't know what to do in the face of it. I tried so hard to fit myself into the shape of someone you could truly love. I did everything I could do. I'm sorry I had to leave you, but I thought you understood. This weekend is actually an opportunity for us to grab a little happiness and you have ignored it. You have ignored me. I said I'd chase you, but I don't see why I should. Am I the only one who cares?

I think I'm angry with you, Alice. It's an uncomfortable sensation. I don't want to get used to it. I like loving you.

Daniel

29th March
The Studio

Dear Alice –

Mab, Freya, and Aubrey arrived yesterday.

Aubrey once told me about a homeless woman he used to look out for in Hong Kong – don't ask what he was doing there, but isn't it like him? This woman used to wear all the clothes she owned at all times. She would creep along the

136

harbour paths, surrounded by sweating tourists and sleek businessmen, spherical in her woollen wadding. The only sign of the scrap of flesh that was herself a tiny grinning grubby face, topped with a collection of hats. I thought of that story as I greeted my sister at the door. The only difference was a tumble of hair instead of the hats.

Freya emerged from behind her mother like a vision. Oh, Alice, I am old. Where I remembered a scruffy little girl there was, in her place, a sleek young woman with a head of glossy hair she habitually and confidently tossed over her shoulder as a colt throws its head. She really does glow. She is a beauty.

'Uncle Dan!' The tiniest trace of an accent. Freya opened her long brown arms to me and tried for an embrace. I'm so big it would have taken three of her to circle me. Her scent was light and warm as her laugh. She really did seem delighted to see me.

'Grandpa! Is this wonderful Tatty Dog I've heard so much about?' She left me with the pressure of her kiss on my cheek and some smear of coloured lip grease I didn't have the heart to scrub from my skin.

Aubrey just looked like Aubrey.

You will be able to tell by this letter that I have decided to forgive you. You have been understanding about my absence; I must learn to be understanding about yours. So, instead of you actually being here, I will help you imagine you are by my side. I'm going to try to detail everything that happens.

We're all together now in the living room. Mab's taken my chair by the fire with Freya arranged prettily on the rug at her feet, playing with Tatty, and Aubrey is in Dad's evening chair, so I'm perched on the edge of Dad's bed. Dad's still sitting in front of the TV, even though it's been turned off; he keeps turning round and trying to join in the conversation, but the wings of his armchair are hindering him. Mab and Aubrey are doing a pretty good job of ignoring Dad's existence and mine, which seems a bit rich considering Dad's the reason they're here and if it weren't for me there wouldn't even be an exhibition. In fact they seem kind of cosy, together in front of the fire. It's as if they're plotting something.

I was going to write about what a consolation Freya has been, and then she turned to Mab and started chattering away in French. Then, would you believe it, Aubrey joined in. I am the picture of ignorance.

It feels a little like it used to when Mab came for the summer holidays. I'm forced into seeing the studio through a stranger's eyes. Aren't guests always strangers when they first arrive? The place looks grubby and ill-used; Maggie tried to work her magic but claimed there were too many feet under hers and gave up. Personally, I feel invaded. It's not where I want to be, but it's my place.

Night-time arrangements have been just as awkward. For some reason, Mab and Freya had to have my room and Aubrey is in the tiny first-floor bedroom on a blow-up mattress. I set up the remaining old cot in the studio for myself and got the blow-heaters running to keep it warm. The sounds are all different here. Next door's trees with all their bluster are on the wrong side. The floor creaks as if someone is constantly creeping across the boards towards me. I slept badly and told everyone I slept well. In fact, I dreamt I was at sea – easy reading for that one, Mr Freud –

on a storm-tossed boat chasing up and down gigantic waves. At one o'clock in the morning I had to run downstairs to empty my bowels in an ugly rush and sat there for a good ten minutes wondering if I could make it back up to my bed. Don't they say worse things happen at sea?

I might try to smuggle Tatty up the stairs with me tonight. Her neat round weight can be a great comfort. That's if I can pull her away from the warmth of the fire and Dad. I'm worried no one seems to have really considered Dad's role in the exhibition. I'm surprised to find myself feeling protective of him. As Mab, Freya and Aubrey talk, I watch Dad. Back in the bad times when I finally got to Corsica, and actually for all those years in Manchester, I didn't think I'd ever be able to forgive him. And I knew he would never forgive me. But sitting here now, where we are both ignored in our own house, I find myself in affinity with him.

When he found me with Sarah it was as if I had never really seen his face before. You know how the faces of those you love are so familiar they drift into a kind of soup of features? Dad was just Dad. Indescribable as anything else. That night he introduced himself piece by piece. Fist by fist and boot by boot, he killed my father as he tried to kill me. He would hate that I am here.

While he beat me I thought of my mother. The woman I cannot remember. I thought that finally I understood what she felt as she dove into that river of traffic and off the footbridge where her son waited for her with the homeless man. I imagined the sensation of finally meeting the wheels of the cars which darted, quick fish, below us. The wheels turned like waves, crushing and pounding the asphalt until it cracked and burst and men from the council had to come and erect plastic barriers and draw chalk lines around the potholes as if they were murder victims. Those wheels burst my mother open. They surrendered her to the detritus of the road, to take her place alongside the crisp packets and fag ends and pieces of broken hubcap along its wasted shoreline. Her indigestible parts.

(Later)

A conversation with Mab:

'Why are you sulking?'

'I'm thinking.'

'Don't do that, Dan. Bad for your health. What are you scribbling there?'

'It's nothing.'

'More dirty little notes? I hope you're being sensible.'

'What do you mean?'

'Just that.'

'Have you said goodnight to Dad?'

'Is it really worth it? He's hardly going to notice. I've seen him all right. That's enough for now.'

'You've not said two words to him since you got here.'

'Well, he doesn't seem to be in a chatty mood. I do my part, Daniel. That's all any of us can do, isn't it? Play our parts.'

'And the weekend? What happens then?'

'Oh, Michael will be fine for that. I've got a friend with a wheelchair we can use. We'll sit him in the corner with a drink and he can shake people's hands and they'll say what a good listener he is and tell him all about his own work. That's how these things go. You just make sure you keep your head down. I don't want any trouble, Dan.'

'Trouble? Jesus, Mab! Who do you think it was who organised all this? Who do you think made all this happen?'

'Oh, do stop shouting. We all know who's in charge. Just quieten down or you'll wake the house.'

'Has Freya gone up to bed already? I wanted to say goodnight.'

'My daughter is off limits, Dan. Let's make that understood right now. Freya is to be left alone. It's enough that you convinced her she needed to be here. It's enough that I've brought her here; that I passed on your notes. God, look who I'm talking to. No trouble, Danny, just remember that.'

I think Mab is more worried about the mask performance than she wants to admit. I did offer to take over the organisation for her, but she just snapped at me. She seems so distracted and preoccupied. Maybe all these years as a single parent have worn her down. She certainly seems confused, I mean, who tells a person to stop shouting and then yells at them?

Love me better, Alice.

Your Daniel

31st March
The Workhouse

Dear Alice –

We sit in front of a lit stage, watching the occasional figure in black trousers and black polo-neck cross the floor with frowning intent but no apparent purpose. Mab has taken her place on the front row. I can see her brushing her wild hair out of her eyes. She's knelt over the back of her chair talking to a similarly wrapped and draped woman, who was introduced to me earlier as an up-and-coming sculptor from Croydon. Mab sees me watching her and winks. At least she seems to have cheered up. Then I realise Freya is sitting a couple of rows behind me. Perhaps the wink was for her?

The drinks were served early and the audience is loud and informal. They all twist round in their chairs, glass stems between loose fingers, and talk and laugh and complain. Reassuring themselves, with furtive glances around the room, that every other guest is as recognisable and as important as they consider themselves to be.

This is quite a novelty for them. For once they don't have to worry about the possibility of a better party across town. They are stranded here. There is nowhere else to be. They are ready to be entertained by whatever comes their way.

The one silent spot in this busy hall is settled over Aubrey and me. Even Freya is busy with a crowd of admirers – all shopping for a new muse, no doubt. I'd like to be able to intervene and protect her, but the flow of people through the room seems to conspire against my interference. I sit writing to you with Aubrey beside me. He keeps trying to enter the conversations around us with his standard smile and bluster, but nothing sticks. It's really quite funny to watch. He even turns to me in the hope of starting something of his own, but I absorb myself in writing. I won't play. He's looking at the stage now. The only one in the room to do so. He's forgotten to stop smiling.

One of the polo-shirts is making his way to the light switch by the door. There's some coughing and scraping of chairs. Prosecco is being tipped down throats all around me, as they ready themselves for the show. They're more attentive than I thought.

(Later)

So, as you're not here, I must bring the show to you. To be honest I'm grateful for a chance to escape the party. They've cleared the chairs away now and the drinking has begun again in earnest. Someone's thought to set up a CD player and there's some soothing classical mix playing, but the atmosphere is more like that of a house party or a wedding reception disco. I've found a quiet corner, behind one of the improvised wings, where I can watch and record without being disturbed.

The actors circulate with their masks slung over their hands, like waiters with unusual platters. Their effect on the crowd seems greater than that of the alcohol. I just saw a man in a three-piece suit conduct a long, animated conversation with one leering half-mask, while the actor holding it kept up the mask's end with shifts of his hand to mimic nods and querying tilts. There is too much laughter and it's all too loud. Something has been shaken loose. This night will last till dawn.

The performance started with one Mask on the stage. This one was a talker. It surprised me, because Mab had warned me that Masks usually have to be taught to speak. This one babbled on, moving across the stage swiftly and with great confidence, but still with the air of something otherworldly in the rigid features frozen above his wet and mobile mouth. He played with the audience, fondling one man's tie and then stealing a woman's scarf and knotting it carefully around his own wrist. He laughed at their faces and mocked them roundly. But it was all very good-natured. The victims seemed delighted by his attentions and I saw others shifting forward in their seats, hoping to be among the chosen. The mask itself was a good one, half-face, heavy-nosed and heavy-lidded. The actor had taken on a foreign accent of some description and he couldn't seem to stand still. It was all strangely captivating. Like watching a man go mad and being allowed to laugh at him.

Before our interest could wane, the Mask introduced a friend. A new actor – a middle-aged woman who rivalled Maggie and myself for girth – was helped into her mask and then given a flash of her reflection in a hand mirror. It was a full-face mask, the mouth a tiny pout and painted wide dark eyes. She made no sound, but pulled her body up and minced around, her hands fluttering before her. The audience cooed and she gifted them a curtsey. One of the black polo-necks trailed her to the edge of the stage, occasionally flashing her a glimpse in the mirror, which she fed off like Narcissus at his pool until it was cut away. The male Mask tried to engage her, but she had found a plastic flower on the prop table and was busy trying to plant it, bloom first, in between the feet of the first row. She sat cross-legged, making a loop out of a lock of her hair, and thrusting the plastic stem of her flower between patent shoes. She was so innocent and so beautiful. And also, strangely, familiar.

Laughter told me that a third Mask had arrived and I was aware of a new barked voice on the stage, but I couldn't stop watching the woman. She was still at play on the edge of the stage and seemed completely self-absorbed. She had found a cloth doll knocked off the prop table and was dancing it around. It was possible to forget that her face was made of clay and shaped by my sister's fingers. As it tilted and shifted in the light, it seemed to live and breathe and move. I was sure that expressions were made and lost. It was an extraordinary piece of work.

I couldn't tell you how long the performance went on for, or how long I sat there mesmerised by her and her doll. She was complete in her own performance. She didn't do much, but what she did was so uninhibited and natural I could have watched all evening. In her purity, she had a kind of magnetism. Oh, it's so hard to describe! I wanted to be near her; to feel her; to feel what she was feeling.

It wasn't until the third Mask approached and snatched her toy that I realised I recognised him. It was *my* mask. The mask Mab sent me. She must have taken it from my bedroom wall. The mask himself was really quite an aggressive and brutal creature. The audience chased him back with the noise of their collective displeasure. He sat and sulked on his haunches at the back of the stage, until the main Mask tried to draw him into another game with a reviving flash of a mirror. This involved some crude business with the female Mask's doll. Cue much leering and unseemly gestures from the third Mask and then, I think, the talker beat him with a rubber stick. I'm sure there was some sort of story going on, but I didn't really follow it.

It was such a shock to see someone else wearing my mask. I almost stood up from my seat to reclaim it. The actor was obviously some stooge. He had none of the honesty of the other Masks. He was just going through the motions. Playing a part. Turning the whole event into a pantomime. Of course the rest of the crowd ate it up.

Still, I must admit, watching my mask move without me behind it was absorbing. I kept twisting in my seat to try and catch Mab's attention, but the vacancy of his face drew me back to the stage. The other masks were luridly painted and stylised; mine was blank clay from brow to chin. He offered the eyes nothing to catch hold of and remember.

I hated the end. One of the polo-necks, an older grey-haired one, who I suppose was the director, ordered the masks removed. The actors simply slipped them off and into the waiting hands of other assistants. There was a short moment of adjustment and then they stood together to receive applause. It was awful. Reality was back, the illusion of the sweet child and the monster lost forever. I mourned it.

No one else seemed affected. They all clapped and shouted praise, their flushed faces open to the stage now full of nothing but predictably preening actors. I blame the booze.

After the show, I tried to find Mab. I wanted to know what she was up to with the masks. Instead, I found myself speaking to the middle-aged woman who had affected me in her Mask incarnation. She'd changed out of her plain black clothes and was now dressed in some kind of large purple smock with lines of glitter running through it. She had also made up her face, perhaps to compensate for its banality.

'I'm afraid I don't remember much of the performance. You'll know better than I what I did. It's always that way when the Mask takes hold. I'd not worked with Her before, but I shall again. That's if your sister will let me.'

She laughed. She had lipstick on her teeth. She was already looking around for someone else to talk to. The woman was an idiot. I wish I'd never spoken to her.

I thought I saw Freya and her flicking hair in the crowd, but she was lost behind a row of black-suited backs. I don't know what trouble Mab thinks I could cause, but with her daughter throwing her charms at every man in the room she needs someone to look after her interests. She's the real troublemaker, if only Mab could see it.

There was one other strange thing in this strangest of evenings. As I was looking for Freya, I realised the fat lady Mask was watching me again, and with none of the indifference she had displayed during our short conversation. She was looking from me to my Mask. My Mask was carried by one of the actors, just like the others. But, unlike the others, the crowd seemed to avoid rather than gather around it, and its support was looking bored and as though he had drunk too much prosecco. Still, the fat lady looked from me to the blank face in his hand. Stupid, I know, but I could have been sure she knew we were connected. And for some reason she looked terrified.

I'll write again tomorrow for the big event,

Daniel

1st April
The Studio

Dear Alice –

It's the morning of the exhibition. I thought I'd write and post this off before we get to the workhouse. That way you can have my day in instalments and I won't forget to write anything down.

Heads were pretty heavy after the Mask show last night. I don't know what time Freya and Mab got back, but Aubrey and I didn't leave until the early hours and the party was still going strong. Maggie is in a bad mood about missing it all, so turned up early and started banging about until I got up and quietened her. Dad, of course, was oblivious, seated on the edge of his bed in his long johns and T-shirt watching Maggie move things. And Sarah was sitting next to him, stroking the side of his face with her hand. She must have come in with Maggie.

'I missed you at the show last night,' I said.

'I couldn't make it. Thought I'd spend the time with your dad instead.' She wouldn't look at me. Her hand trembled.

'If you're going to mess with his face like that, you should try the other side. The stroke ruined the feeling on his right.'

For no real reason, I was angry with her. I went through to the kitchen to make tea. By the time I got back the rest of the house was up: Aubrey already buttoned into his three-piece suit, looking in want of a pipe; Mab chain-smoking in an extraordinary pair of pyjamas; and Freya picking her way through it all like a ballerina, her hair tied into a knot on the top of her head. She smiled at me and took my hand briefly as she wished me good morning. Obviously nothing has been said about her behaviour last night. Still, I'm not her parent. I smiled back.

We managed to get through the business of breakfast. Mab took numerous calls on her mobile, which appeared to consist mostly of hectic laughter and complaints about the phone reception. I'd taken it that the crowd who turned up last night were all of the invitees to today's exhibition, but it seemed that people were still arriving. London was flowing into Upchurch without any sense of direction. I fielded calls on the landline and persuaded people not to visit us at home.

I let Maggie and Sarah sort Dad out. Thankfully, the wheelchair idea of Mab's appears to have been forgotten and Dad looks quite respectable in one of his old suits, despite the weight he has lost. Sarah has bought him a pale blue shirt for the occasion. Freya said how well it brought out his eyes, when Maggie and Sarah brought him through from the bathroom and turned him round in the centre of the crowded living room.

I think dressing him this early a mistake, but it looks as though Maggie and Sarah are willing to take on babysitting him. I'm certainly glad of the freedom. If I can just shake loose from Aubrey, it could be a good evening.

(Later)

Despite my best efforts, we have had visitors. Claggy, the agent, brought them round. Two men in expensive coats and a glossy-lipped, grey-haired woman of indeterminate age. I was foolish to have doubted Sarah and Maggie's preparations, because of course Dad is the major exhibit for this show.

Claggy led them round like a tour guide, pointing out possible areas of interest. When they got to Dad, for one strange moment I thought they might actually kneel and kiss his hand. Actually Dad did rather well: he looked up at them and didn't screech or holler the way he did last time Claggy was here. I think I saw her cross her fingers behind her back as they approached him.

Sarah sat at Dad's elbow like a courtesan, her hand on his shoulder. She seemed to calm him. In fact, she always seems to calm him. I've been trying to make sense of their relationship for most of my life. I'm still no closer to an answer. I just know enough to realise that any affection Sarah once had for me has disappeared. Gone and never to be recovered.

After their audience with Dad, the visitors trooped out into the garden to look at the choked and muddy pond, Aubrey and Freya on hand with the full charm offensive. I went into the kitchen with Maggie to fetch tea and 'best biscuits', which she'd picked up from a shop in town especially in case of guests. It was then that I noticed Maggie had made rather an effort. She was dressed in a smart blue wool dress with a hideous brooch on her left breast which I had never seen before. I suspected it was a treasure. There was even the suggestion of lipstick around her mouth.

'You look lovely,' I said, wrapping an arm around her middle as best I could.

'Nonsense.' She blushed and patted at her hair. Pleased. 'Now get your hands off me. I'll upset the biscuits. Make yourself useful and go and fetch your sister. Don't think I didn't see her scurry off, just when she's needed. And leave off those, they're for that lot outside.'

I went through to the living room, passing Dad still sitting in state. I fed the last bite of my best biscuit to Tatty and climbed the stairs.

So, I forgot to knock. So, I caught Mab just as she was stepping out of her pyjamas and into her underwear. So, I saw my sister naked. I don't know why it needed to be made such a fuss over. It's not as though it was the first time I'd ever seen her without her clothes on

I will write again when we arrive.

Daniel

1st April
The exhibition

Dear Alice –

A man and woman are standing in front of the largest of Dad's portraits. They tilt their heads and take small steps back and forth. The woman has a sweep of pale blonde hair that she fusses with, reaching up a hand to flip it over her shoulder and away from her face. I suspect her of meeting Freya on her way in. The couple exchange a few words, but it is not entirely clear whether they are together for any other time than these few moments in front of the painting. They both hold wine glasses and the dregs of their champagne. The man has a soiled napkin crushed in his fist.

A louder group approaches – jostling suits and a woman in a scarlet dress. The couple move away. The man towards a cluster of smaller frames, and the blonde woman – head raised – into the centre of the room, looking to catch the arm of a circulating waiter.

There was music when we arrived, some kind of jazz piped so softly it was impossible to identify. Our party arrived ten minutes late as Mab had instructed. She said the artist should always be the last to arrive. We got Dad through the crowd and over to a group of chairs in a far corner. Sarah sat down beside him to do the talking and the smiling. I leant over to whisper a warning about letting people get too close to him and she flinched away from me. I wonder what lies she's been fed in my absence. Mab seemed as sick of her as I was and went off to talk to the catering staff. It was only then that I turned and saw the room.

It had been transformed. The portraits were all hung according to Dad's preferred style: some in isolation; some arranged above each other in irregularly shaped groups. All the canvases were draped in individual dust sheets – which I thought a little extreme – and were to be revealed one at a time as Mab gave a short introduction from the improvised stage. Yes, another section of the evening where my dear sister has decided to wrest control away from me.

The swathed frames served the purpose of extenuating the architecture of the hall. The red-brick walls looked somehow brighter and the white-painted window frames swallowed their dark panes. They must have done something to the lights. Waiters were already moving through the crowd of guests with canapés and glasses of champagne and there were white-sheeted tables from which people could help themselves. Most of the crowd I recognised from last night, but they were glossy and well-dressed. I felt scruffy in my shirt and jeans. The clack of high heels and polished brogues almost drowned out the music. They would probably take me for staff, or whatever comes below staff at this kind of event.

Aubrey also seemed strangely out of his element, and as reluctant to leave my side as he had been the night before. Not really his kind of crowd, I assume. All too happy and able to take care of themselves.

Mab did a pretty good job with the introduction to the paintings, though the constant unveiling quickly became tedious and some of the portraits were pulled out of line as they pulled the dust sheets free. She didn't mention my name when the largest painting of me came up, but gave it a title, *Honoured with Human Shape*, which I didn't understand. I was hoping, at the very least, for a personal spotlight and a short round of applause. But that may have been in some part due to the quantity of champagne I'd consumed. There were a lot of strange titles which I'd never heard before – mostly quotes from Shakespeare. Mab must have found them in Dad's notebooks.

I'm missing you. No one wants to talk to me. They're more interested in being in the vague vicinity of Dad, even as he dribbles down his new shirt. Even Maggie has an audience – she's wrestled a tray of vol-au-vents from one of the waiters and is feeding them to a group of actors as if she baked them herself. No one knows my connection to Dad, so no one wants to know me. I'm amazed that no one recognises me, despite my face being on nearly every wall. I've been sitting at the corner of this table for over an hour and not one person has interrupted or questioned my writing. Perhaps they think I'm a journalist? But then, I've never been very good at judging what people see when they look at me.

I watch people approach the biggest portrait. It is hung on the east wall, bracketed by two minor sketches behind glass. It's one I had examined only briefly when I stacked it against the studio wall. I don't even remember packing it for the exhibition. It looks larger and more imposing hung against red brick. The coils and sweeps of oil paint catch the light and look still wet. It is certainly my face, but dashed at and exaggerated by my father's brush so as to look almost monstrous. Is this what my father saw when he remembered me?

Of course the crowd are, despite their gloomy attitude, most comfortable with the Sarah portraits. Mab says she's gathered a number of offers from collectors who already possess Sarah's body as a Submerged Nude. Although there has been talk of taking the whole collection down to London for an exhibition-run before any sales are made. But he – my *doppelgänger* – is drawing some attention. I don't think anyone is interested in owning my portraits, but they don't seem to be able to stop looking at them.

'Oh, will you look at this one.'

'Bloody hell! He's hideous.'

'I don't know. There's something about him I rather like.'

'You would. He reminds me of your ex.'

'You two have found the Caliban, then. He's remarkable, isn't he? I didn't know Laird had a *him* in him, if you follow me.'

'I know! All that talk of him hating women and it turns out he knows exactly how to hate men.'

'Talking from experience, are we, darling?'

'I'm not saying I know a lot about Art and all that, but I like him. It's the eyes. There's something sad about the eyes. As if he's done terrible things, seen terrible things, but it's not his fault. Does that make sense?'

'I told you, you should have stopped at the second glass. Come away, I want to see the self-portraits.'

'Just give me a couple of minutes. I'll catch you up.'

I should go and talk to her, the woman in front of my portrait. She's just my type. It would be so easy. All I'd have to do is go and stand next to the painting, show her my sad eyes. But she's more than a little drunk and she's not you, Alice. You're the one I want to trust me. You're the one I want to take me home.

The whole lot of them are pretty drunk now. The music has been turned up and Django Reinhardt is playing. I watch Mab stagger into the caterer's set-up room and come out holding another crate of champagne aloft. People rush forward and break the corks from the bottles themselves, laughing over the noise and froth. The waiters stand back and smile, as if this is a normal turn of events. Mab comes over and swipes a kiss on to my cheek. 'Behaving yourself?' They are all having a wonderful time.

I take a tour of the room. Spot Aubrey deep in conversation with a dark-haired woman in green high-heels. His hand is on her shoulder and he has his professional face on. I wouldn't be surprised if he's charging her by the hour. The extra drink is taking effect. A man falls back into a large self-portrait and sets it swinging. He is helped up and out by two discreet men in suits. I suppose Mab must have hired security without telling me. Another thing I suppose I should have thought of myself. At least the painting is undamaged.

I find myself in front of one of the Sarah portraits. This is one I haven't seen before. It must have been from the damaged and bound-together lot I sent off to Claggy's restorer. This portrait is closer to the Sarah I knew than any of the others. She looks young and beautiful, but the expression is extraordinary. Her hands reach up to her face, one grasping a claw full of hair. She is despair. It's as if unhappiness has never been painted before. I didn't know she could look like that. The strangest thing is – the longer I stare at it – the shadow of familiarity I feel. Like a long-forgotten memory. I suppose it is well known that painters often corrupt their portraits with an image of their own features transposed across that of their sitter. There is no greater narcissist than the artist. But this is different. Behind the misery in Sarah's face I think I recognise a younger Mab, and then maybe even you.

Just as I think I'm making sense of it, just when I'm coming to the edge of deciding how I feel about it all, a woman steps back from a laughing group on to my heel.

'Oh, I'm so sorry!' we both say at once.

It's Freya.

'Isn't it a fabulous party?' She staggers and laughs, revealing her tiny white teeth. There's a glass of something fizzy in her hand. I wonder if she's drinking champagne. She's wearing a spill of dark grey silk, fastened at the shoulders with sliver clasps. I can see her nipples, hard under the dress, and find myself imagining the rest of her lithe body beneath the fabric. Her taut brown skin and my lips against it. Maybe *I'm* a little drunk.

Not that I'd ever do anything, of course. No matter how she provokes me or how much champagne they pour down my throat. Don't be jealous. You are my girl, Alice. My one and only girl.

But, it is her hand that's on my arm. 'I'm so proud of Grandpa. And of Ma, of course. Everyone's talking about them. Everyone seems to know them, and to want to know me.' She leans in close to my ear. I can smell her breath and the taint of alcohol. 'You know, I love it! Does that make me very vain? Or just very lonely?'

She spins on her heels as a hand reaches out from the group behind her and catches her round the waist. Her short dress gathers and I get a flash of her white schoolgirl knickers before she turns and joins the throng of the young and beautiful. I wonder if she even recognised me.

I needed to see Dad. This morning seemed an age away and I realised I hadn't checked on him since the beginning of the exhibition. I found him still in his chair, a half-empty bottle of whisky and a glass on the small table beside him. A large man in a bright waistcoat was talking loudly at him, apparently oblivious to the lack of reply. Mab was next to Dad, her feet slung over the side of her seat as she chatted to a group of the actors from last night's show. Sarah was nowhere to be seen. I ignored the waistcoat man and leant down to check Dad's catheter bag. Taut and full. The bottom of his trouser leg was damp with urine. I got him to his feet to help him towards the bathroom where we could sort him out. He put his hand on my shoulder as I lifted him. I actually could have believed he was pleased to see me. It was probably the whisky.

'Can I help with him?' It was Sarah. Her features looked sort of blurred. It could have been the effect of too much champagne, or the fact that her face was staring out of the walls around us.

'I'm fine. I'm used to it. Stay. Enjoy the party.' It was my turn to walk away from her. It felt rather good.

'It's not a party, Daniel. It's an appreciation of Michael's work. And I can take him home if he needs to go.'

'I'm just taking him to the Gents. I don't think you can really help there. And this crowd are hardly ready to appreciate the most basic functions of the great artist. Apparently that's my job.'

We got away from her. It was the most normal exchange we'd had since I returned to Upchurch and it was full of hostility. I half-dragged Dad across the room to the stairs. He turned in my arms at one point to look back at Sarah. She waved and blew a kiss. The whole thing was sickening.

I'll write again when we get home,

Your Daniel

2nd April
My prison cell

Dear Alice –

Apparently I shouldn't be writing this, but what else can I do? I don't understand what's going on. I'm in a fucking prison cell, Alice, and apparently I have you to thank. There must have been some mistake. You're lying. I don't know why you're lying. But you are lying.

The party was coming to a close as I brought Dad back from the toilet. The few guests that remained were trying to keep the frivolity going with the last bottles of champagne, but their laughter was getting hard and forced. Mab came over to Dad and me, taking hold of Dad's other arm.

'Better get going soon,' she whispered to me, still smiling at people as we passed. 'It's going to get ugly if we don't cut it short. I've just got to find that daughter of mine. Thundering success, though, Pops. Well done you.' She patted Dad's arm and moved away.

Sarah was waiting for us by the chairs. The fat man in the waistcoat was still there.

'Where did you get to? You've been gone for ages. Come here, Michael, there's someone bursting to meet you. Thank you, Daniel.'

I was dismissed. Just like that.

I stood for a moment watching Sarah ease Dad back into his seat. I remember the music was playing and it was the Django Reinhardt compilation going round again and I thought maybe they only have the one CD and why haven't I noticed until now? I was looking for Freya, hoping we could get some time on our own, when I saw the woman. Her lips were stained with red wine and her make-up slightly smeared. She paused mid-conversation. She seemed to be looking right at me. Fascinated. She raised the glass in her hand, a parody of a toast, and instinctively I raised my own. But then I realised she was actually groping for her companion's back. Trying to attract his attention, without taking her eyes off me. I smiled awkwardly.

It was then that the hand dropped on to my shoulder. They actually do that: put the hand on your shoulder when they come to arrest you.

'Daniel Laird?'

'Yes?'

'Daniel Laird of 1 Church Street, Upchurch? Formerly of Grey Lanes, Manchester?'

'That's right.'

'We're going to need you to come with us, sir.'

My arresting officer was a woman, short and attractive, but bulky in her uniform. My first thought was that Mab had arranged a stripper for the close of the exhibition. I imagined her peeling off her uniform piece by piece. I must have grinned. Such a cliché! I thought the whole thing was a joke. Then the second policeman stepped forward. They looked so neat and well put together in their smart uniforms. Especially when compared to the last of the party goers. It must have been the start of their shift.

They didn't use handcuffs. I must have looked pretty docile, but I think it would have felt more real with handcuffs. People stopped and stared at us as we passed through the room to the door. I couldn't see anyone I knew. Sarah and Dad were behind me. As far as I could tell, they were still carrying on their conversation with the man in the waistcoat. I looked for Mab and Freya but there was no sign of them. Strange. The thought I had was to ask if Freya could come with me in the car, as if it were an ambulance ride and I needed a companion for the journey.

A hand to hold to take away the pain. Instead, it was the portraits that accompanied me to the police car. Their eyes averted.

They sat me in the back of the car. The female police officer held the door open for me, but I don't remember her guiding my head in through it. Maybe she did. The police car smelt of rubber and air-freshener. It was like being in a taxi. I wasn't sure whether to put my seatbelt on or not. I had that same compulsion to talk that one gets in the back of a cab. I leant forward and the female officer told me to sit back. She kept calling me *sir* or *Mr Laird*. I wanted to ask her to call me Daniel. Their radios buzzed and whistled and the two of them conversed in quiet voices. They even laughed. They seemed to have forgotten all about me.

Can you imagine what I felt when they read me those charges? When they said those things about me, the things I was meant to have done to you? And for you to have been the one who went and reported it as if it were fact...

Rape and aggravated harassment.

There were statutes and sections and acts all referenced in the charges. None of which I understood. None of which seemed to have anything to do with me. What could I have done, my darling Alice, to make you so angry with me? Why are you telling such terrible lies?

You must phone the police and explain your mistake.

Daniel

2nd April
My prison cell

Dear Mab –

This is a hideous place to be writing from. I keep bursting into tears, just like my Alice. I can't believe she has done this to me. I told you she was angry about my abandoning her, but even I had no idea she would go to such extremes to make me take notice of her. Well, she's got my fucking attention now.

This cell is small and white. There's a kind of shelf on the back wall with a thin foam mattress covered in shiny plastic, I suppose so one can piss oneself without causing any great damage. The smell is soiled, but overlaid with detergent. It makes me think of Maggie. I should be glad I don't have to shit in a bucket. In fact, I just knock on the metal door and they take me down the corridor. I busy myself by reading the walls. There have been a lot of angry people in this cell before me. The walls are white-painted breeze blocks, and men – I'm presuming men – have carved or painted their threats and despairs all over them.

DEVON'S A SNITCH

fuck you bitch

I WILL KILL YOU MATT YOU FUCKING LIER

SCREW YOU PIG

… and one large INNOCENT scrawled across the right-hand wall.

I don't know how they got the materials to write. The policeman took my shoes off me as I entered the cell, so that I couldn't hang myself with the laces. Apparently they are less concerned about blades and biros.

I am INNOCENT, Mab. Read the writing on the wall. You have to get me out of here. I don't know how it works. I asked for a lawyer and they stuck me in here to wait for the duty solicitor. Should I have just gone into the interview alone? Surely you know someone who is better than any solicitor they will provide? Maybe Aubrey will help? Do I need someone to post bail, or is that just on cop shows? It's a bit scary that my only frame of reference for my present situation is stuff I've seen on Dad's TV.

Help me, Mab.

Daniel

3rd April
My prison cell

Dear Mab –

Policeman: Right, we have a great deal of information here. Ms Williams' claims of sexual assault and harassment appear to be borne out not only by the letters you sent her, but by your own accounts given here. Of course, you claim that any sexual acts were entirely consensual.

[PAUSE]

For the tape, please, Mr Laird.

Me: Yes. I mean, I nodded. That's true. In fact she – Alice – instigated some of them. She was angry when I left her. She –

P/M: Ms Williams was angry? And how did she express this anger?

Me: She wouldn't write to me. I invited her to my father's exhibition and she didn't come.

P/M: Couldn't this silence be interpreted as a refusal to conduct any kind of a relationship with you?

Me: Of course we 'conducted a relationship'. Do you think I'm crazy? It was just a game of hers. She wanted me to come home.

P/M: So, again I must ask you how she expressed this wish. Was there any conversation or communication between you that could be construed as encouraging your advances?

Me: It was everything. She loved me. She told me that she loved me all the time. Or rather, it was one of those things she never had to say. From the first time we met –

P/M: That was outside the offices of the therapist who employs you as his... assistant. Is that right?

Me: Yes. Aubrey. He was here, wasn't he? He can tell you. I mean, she was obviously far more unstable than I realised. She was seeing a therapist, for Christ's sake. She might have been taking medication. Maybe she should have been taking medication.

[PAUSE]

Anyway, she started talking to me. Of course I was there. My boss works there. It's not as though I was waiting for her. She wanted a cigarette and we talked. We had a connection. That's where it all started.

P/M: Yet Ms Williams claims not to remember exchanging more than a few words with you before the first alleged assault.

Me: I'm the victim here. She's the crazy one. I would never do anything like this… this… horrible thing she's accusing me of. I didn't rape her. I didn't harass her. I was in love with her. Is that a crime?

[PAUSE]

I'm not a criminal. You've had half my family in here talking to you. They'll tell you. They can explain.

P/M: As you say, Mr Laird. However, if we return to the letter dated 23rd January. That would be directly following the second alleged assault?

Me: There was no assault. We spent the night together. Why do you have those letters? They were for Alice. They're not meant to be read by anyone but Alice.

P/M: Ms Williams passed us these as evidence of your stalking. This has been explained to you. And I can't help but note, when we asked you for any evidence of her correspondence you were unable to provide anything. And found within your possessions were these photographs –

Me: Those are private! They are nothing! I mean – they are proof of our love for each other. How dare you sully them with the idea –

P/M: Isn't it in fact true that, until your invitation to this exhibition, Ms Williams didn't have any idea where you were living or where the letters were coming from? For the record, this was the same letter in which you threaten the victim with further assault. Threats which finally led Ms Williams to contact the authorities.

Me: I was upset because she wasn't coming to the show, that's all. All couples argue over silly things like that. She didn't need to write to me. She didn't need to say or do anything. We were in love. She loved me. That was all I needed to know.

Daniel

5th April
The Studio

Dear Aubrey –

Yes, they let me out. I don't know what you told the police, but I think I owe you a debt of gratitude. You must have been very convincing.

It really has been the most horrible time. I'm actually grateful to be back with Dad and Tatty. It must have been worse than I thought.

Mab collected me yesterday and brought me back before heading to London. She seemed annoyed with me. As if I'd orchestrated the whole business to embarrass her. But most of the guests had left by the time the policemen came to get me, and I think those who remained had enough champagne in them to be convinced it was some kind of elaborate joke. I certainly don't see why I should be blamed, let alone subjected to the silent treatment Mab gave me on the journey back from the police station.

When I asked after Freya she actually turned on me with genuine anger.

'You've learnt nothing from this, have you, Dan? Well, I have. I don't know why I ever let myself be talked into bringing my girl here. Why I ever let her near you. I suppose I thought – I hoped – that even you wouldn't go there with a member of your own family. I think I actually started to believe the lies I've been telling for all these years – believe you could actually change. But I remember, Danny. I'm a fucking elephant when it comes to you. You can't even see the truth when it's played out in front of your face.

'And I *knew* – you fucking well *told* me – about this new girl! Why didn't I realise? Why didn't I tell that little shit Aubrey?'

Then she burst into tears. We had to pull over while she recovered herself. I don't know what on earth she had to cry about. I'm the one who should be weeping after all I've been through. I suppose she must have heard about Freya's behaviour at Dad's exhibition. I wouldn't have taken Mab for a strict parent, but it's amazing what age can do to change a person. Still, it was sad not to be able to say goodbye to my niece.

Mab was good enough to find me a decent solicitor. Not that he had much to say during the endless interviews or when they were reading my private letters or asking me in graphic detail about the minutiae of my sex life. And don't think I didn't ask. Still, he got me out, though he took great pains to explain every last restriction to my new-found freedom. I am not to write, call, visit or contact Alice in any way. I am to remain at home as much as possible and generally keep my head down until the police decide they want to see me again. I am to report to the local police station once a week, just so they can be sure I am doing or not doing everything they have instructed I do or don't do. It's fucking ridiculous. I'm being punished for something I haven't done; for something Alice decided.

I do wish I could just talk to her. There must be some kind of explanation for her behaviour, though at the moment I'm at a loss to think of one. As for leaving the house, I'm not really in a sociable mood. So far there has been nothing in the papers, but – I'm sure in no small part thanks to Maggie – Upchurch is alive with gossip. Every time I step outside the front door I feel as if someone has hung a sign around my neck with RAPIST written in large, ugly letters.

And talking of large and ugly. Not for the first time, I wish I were smaller and less conspicuous. As far as everyone else is concerned, I have been proved the monster I resemble. How can I fight that, Aubrey?

No, I'm best left here with the silent. Dad and Tatty may not be great conversationalists, but they provide everything I need. Namely, ignorance. I don't think Dad even noticed I'd gone anywhere. It's quite reassuring to be able to step back into life here. Even if I've lost the promise of Alice at the end of it.

Maggie has been strangely absent since my return. I'm not saying I was expecting a welcoming committee, but, what with Mab's reaction to me, I was hoping for some tea and sympathy from Maggie. I haven't seen Sarah either. Since the exhibition weekend, it's as if society has evaporated. I didn't think I'd miss them, but I do. There is no distraction from my thoughts of Alice.

Write to me, Aubrey, or send me some recordings to transcribe or something. I need to believe there is a world outside of this business, and you – God help me – are my great hope.

Yes, I realise this makes me pathetic. There is no reason to elaborate on that in your letter.

Daniel

8th April
The Studio

Dear Freya –

I'm sorry about the horrible confusion at your grandad's exhibition. It's been occupying too much of my time and mind. Rereading the light happiness of your letters to me has been a welcome relief. I did so enjoy receiving them. I'm so glad we got to meet properly and 'connect' (wasn't that the phrase you used?). I'm also so sorry we didn't get to say goodbye properly. Be careful of the nonsense your mother tells you. Don't trust her too much, Freya.

Life is quiet here. Your grandad continues much the same, though I think the business of the exhibition and the influx of people tired him. He seems to have sunk even deeper into himself, if that's possible. Sometimes I forget he is even here.

Tatty and I have found new routes for our walks. I am in no mood for the polite enquiries of other dog-walkers. I have to be careful not to cross too close to any of the farmers' homes. Farmers are not great lovers of dogs on their land or near their livestock. And they have been known to be a little too hasty with the shotgun. We keep to the arable fields.

I was surprised the other day to find a row of crows, butcher-birded on posts, across the middle of one field we crossed. I suppose they were meant to serve as some kind of gruesome warning to other birds to stop them picking at the seeds. I'd seen this phenomenon before from the road, but, short-sightedly, had believed the dead crows to be scraps of black plastic catching the breeze. Tatty appreciated the stench, I think. I did not. The crows in the trees seemed completely indifferent. Though they did keep their distance.

Tell me some tales of Corsica,

Uncle Dan

8th April
The Studio

Dear Mab –

I keep thinking back to our little holiday. That wild stretch of coastline full of wind and salt spray. I know I was stupid enough to run from it, but now it seems it's chasing me. The new routes I take with Tatty remind me of it so. The stark horizon on every side punctuated only by the silhouettes of oak trees, their branches reaching like coral into the sea of the sky. Strange to think it was thoughts of

Alice which haunted me on that holiday. It was thinking of her that eventually drew me away to Manchester and set this whole thing in motion.

The second assault.

All my dreams and hopes and love. Our beautiful night together tainted by those three words. How can she think of anything that happened between us as an assault?

I want to be back on the north Norfolk coast, with all my hopes alive, being hurried and shoved along the long blank sand, Tatty yapping at my feet. I want to take the walk towards the sea at low tide. To follow the lines of debris licked free from the grey sea's tongue. One day we found a great ridge of starfish, no doubt picked clean off some rig during a distant storm at sea. They were perfect, but quite dry and dead. I had trouble keeping Tatty from playing with them. Another day, layer after layer of razor clam shells, which broke and cracked underfoot. I came home with shards stuck into the tread of my boots.

Always towards the sea. Our beach had a black wreck set in the middle distance. The estuary eddied around it, leaving it stranded on a sand bank. It was impossible to reach, but always appeared temptingly close at low tide. The one landmark in the land of horizon. We always walked towards it and then followed the deeper water round to find the ocean.

I clapped my hands to stop Tatty lapping at the shallow wash. Once, on the way back from one of our walks on the beach, she had to stop and vomit wave after wave of salt water on to the brackish marshes. I didn't know her body could hold so much water. Afterwards, she looked so weak that I tried to carry her, but she soon squirmed out of my arms and back on to the sandy path.

Before the sea the wet sand hard, pitted and buckled into pools, peopled by nothing save tiny translucent crabs and the odd scrap of red weed. Further down the coast there is talk of seals and special boat trips out to see them. Here on this winter beach we are alone with the sucking snapping holes of lugworms. Here there is life only if you peer closely. Nothing is obvious but sky and sea.

The sea itself is a surprise when we reach it. Busy with its own flexed muscle, it is entirely indifferent to us. Tatty yaps at the waves a little and then trots back to the pools, chasing some improbable scent. She swats and pisses. The sharp tang of urine snapping back to me in the wind. I stare long and hard, testing my eyes against the ocean's back. Here, a mile from dry land, it waits with perfect patience and feeds on itself.

I've never been that comfortable with being ignored. But there, in my insignificance, I found a kind of peace.

Just longing to be elsewhere,

Daniel

13th April
The Studio

Dear Mab –

Of course I know I shouldn't have sent that letter. To be honest with you, I don't even remember writing it – that day at the police station is pretty much a blur. But yes, I accept it exists and Alice received it. The police made that very clear when they were scaring the life out of me. They convinced me of their unequivocal kindness in letting me go. Apparently, lack of a sexual content finally brought them down on my side. As far on to my side as they are willing to come, that is. I have been strictly warned that any further deviation from the agreed terms and I will be fined and/or incarcerated. It's all very neat and tidy, our legal system. And I'm a part of it now. It doesn't seem to matter that I haven't actually done anything wrong.

It was a moment of weakness, Mab. Writing to Alice is so familiar, so much a part of my life, I suppose I wrote without thinking. And I so much wanted to talk to her and find out what I had done to deserve this. She's obviously angrier than I thought. A part of me had hoped that after the initial arrest she would come to her senses and things would go back to normal. Apparently not.

Maggie came round today. She's decided to pretend nothing has happened. Or at least she started with that line. It turns out the reason she appeared is because it's the district nurse's day to visit and there has been some kind of fuss kicked up about them having to come here while I'm out on bail. I am the sexual predator waiting for innocent nurses to attack in my own home. I can just guess who it was doing the complaining. That bitch nurse has always hated me. I bet she loved telling everyone how right she was. But then Maggie wasn't that much better – seems she couldn't wait to tell me how useless I was being.

'There is dog shit all over this carpet. Have you been taking that Tatty out at all? And look at the state of your dad. I suppose you've just been waiting for me to come and clear up.'

'I've been letting things go a bit, I know.'

'It's a bit more than that, Danny. And don't just sit there feeling sorry for yourself. Get up and help. The nurse will be here in an hour.'

'I don't care about the fucking nurse.'

'Temper, temper. Now look: you're walking it through everywhere. You'd think I'd been gone a month. Get into that kitchen and find some of the good solvent stuff I got you. I'm guessing it hasn't been touched.'

'I'm going. Where have you been, anyway? Suppose you got scared away like the rest of them.'

'Daniel Laird. I changed your nappies, young man. There is nothing you could possibly do to scare me. And if you don't take those filthy boots off this instant I'll be the one scaring you. Hand me that brush and hot water. You get your dad into the bathroom and cleaned and changed. It's a disgrace, is what it is in here.'

I was hauling Dad up out of his seat when she added, 'It was my birthday. I went away for a couple of days with a friend of mine. That's where I was.'

'Oh, Maggie. Why didn't you say anything?'

'Because I didn't want any of this nonsense. And hands off me. I'll be another name on the coppers' list if you carry on like that. Oh, give over with the gloom and doom, Danny. I was only having a joke with you. If you can't laugh, what can you do?'

But she wasn't laughing. If I didn't know her better, I'd have said she looked disgusted.

I suppose I'll have to find some way of getting her a present. Any suggestions for the sadistic old woman who has everything?

Daniel

15th April
The Studio

Dear Mab –

I had to go into town today. Maggie's visit turned out to be a one-off and she didn't bring any supplies with her. We were nearly out of tea and coffee and I'd worked my way to the very back of the food cupboards and freezer drawers. The one thing we had plenty of was whisky, thanks to the couple of cases left over from the exhibition. This has been useful for keeping Dad quiet, but if we were going to eat again I needed to shop.

I'd intended to head for the anonymity of the big supermarket on the bypass, but I was low on petrol and ended up just walking. You know what Upchurch is like. So do I, but I guess I wasn't thinking. In fact, not thinking has been my major pastime for the last few weeks. Or trying not to.

Still, I made it on to the high street all right, before my mind caught up with me.

There seemed to be a fair few people about, despite the overcast day and the rain in the air. It felt as if every single one of them was there to stare at me. The shops were of course familiar, their eyes hooded by faded awnings and lowered beam-work. Clutches of Upchurchers huddled together to talk in doorways or shouted to each other across the street. Not one word for me. I tried to keep my head down, Mab, I really did. But all I could feel was a horrible mix of the panic of my exposure and an utter loneliness. I didn't know whether to run home or throw myself at the feet of the nearest shoppers. They shrugged away from me, as if I were a shark who had swum into a pool of minnows. I have never felt uglier.

When I finally got myself into the baker's, I found I was hardly able to form the words to ask for my sliced loaf. My voice finally thundered out of my throat, chased by a tremor of palpitations. I thought I might pass out and fall on to the worn lino of the shop floor. People could just step over me. The girl behind the counter could slip my order into my bag and gather the right money from the change that spilt from my hands. I thought how cool it would be down there on the floor; how nice it would be to become another unremarkable feature, like the wooden chair by the door that no one ever seemed to sit on. They would close for the night and leave in the dark, with the smell of warm dough, and the next morning I could listen to the girls chatter as they set out the iced buns and re-wiped the surfaces. It would be strange for a while, but they'd soon get used to me. Maybe even fond of me. Inert and low-eyed, the man on the floor, still as a taxidermy and requiring nothing.

I should be used to whispers. Even when I first returned they had enough to occupy their mouths and ears with rumours of me and Sarah. And with what could possibly have happened to make Dad kick me out all those years ago.

It was with those thoughts in my mind that I saw Sarah in the street. I'd managed to get everything I needed and did think of just ignoring her and heading home, but friends at the moment are few and far between. As I've said, I was lonely.

With a smile she dismissed the group of women she was chatting with and stepped back to talk to me.

'Daniel.' Ridiculous, I know, but I still get a thrill from hearing her say my name. 'You're out, then.'

'Just getting some shopping for Dad. Haven't seen you since the business at the exhibition.'

'Yes, well. I spent some time with Michael while you…'

'Were in prison.'

'He seemed really well. He enjoyed himself so much with the comings and goings of the weekend. It was being with people again, I think. It brought out the best in him. It was an amazing night. So nice to see Michael at the centre of everything again. And the paintings looked incredible. I didn't know if I could bear to see them again, but the truth needed to be told, didn't it? That's what those paintings were about: understanding. It's just a shame you don't understand any of it, do you?'

The women she had been talking to had not moved away. They stood as a group at my shoulder and watched us talk. Then one of them leant over to whisper something to Sarah. She did not look at me. Sarah nodded and the woman touched her arm before taking her place back with the other women in the audience.

'Maybe you could explain to me,' I said. 'Do you have time for a cup of tea? I was just heading back now. Dad would be pleased to see you.'

'I can't right now. We've got some things still to do.' She gestured to the waiting women. One of them smiled at her. 'I'll get in touch with Maggie and sort something out for later in the week.'

'You scared to be alone with me too?'

She paused and then looked straight into my face for the first time.

'Yes, Daniel. Of course I am. And don't look so surprised. I'd have to be stupid not to be terrified, wouldn't I?'

The women closed around her in a single movement and Sarah was gone.

I don't know how I got home, but I made it. Dad was hollering about something and pulling at the dressing the nurse put on his arm the other day. Tatty was fussing to go out. I ignored them both and headed for the whisky crate. Half a bottle down and I'm feeling much more peaceful.

All I tried to do was love them, Mab.

Daniel

20th April
The police station

Dear Aubrey –

They've been letting me check in over the phone since the trouble over my letter to Alice. I fed them a line about Dad needing me at home. But I guess I overplayed it, because they insisted I come in person today. I'm waiting to be seen. It seems there is to be another interview. I was hoping it would be a case of signing or stamping something and then sending me home. I can't think that I've done anything wrong, but then I didn't think I'd done anything wrong before. I've certainly not made any contact with Alice. I'm not sure whether that's due to fear of the police or fear of Mab, but it's kept me safe.

It's truly horrible to be back here at the site of all my unhappiness. Not that anyone else is happy to be here either. They've sat me next to a small reception desk on a plastic upholstered chair. There is a policeman behind the desk, studiously avoiding eye contact and occasionally answering the phone. Every now and then someone is brought to be booked in and they either stand with their head hanging while the policemen chat and jolly the odd word out of them, or they kick and swear and the police hold them down and grimace. Those I class as the drunks, but it may be drugs. One girl stood and just cried; she kept repeating 'I'll never do it again' over and over. She looked very young. Another woman broke all my rules by laughing and joking with the man behind the desk and her arresting officers. I classed her a regular. She seemed to know everyone and peered curiously at me. I was glad to be out of place in her world. She looked filthy. She even asked my name. I was tempted to give yours.

(Later)

There is talk of further evidence and proceeding investigations. I am instructed to keep to the house as much as possible and avoiding talking to or disturbing anyone who might be considered a witness. I must say they are very good-natured about the whole thing. I forget of course that this is just their job; they don't actually hate me. But I do wish they'd stop accusing me.

It felt too strange to just leave and go home, so I came back here to my chair by the reception desk. It seems right to be a part of the passing traffic. At least no one here will be called at my trial. *My trial.* It still doesn't seem real. I can't talk to her, but maybe you can do something about Alice? Her address and her number are on file. The records are a little patchy, but if you find anything missing just let me know. Yes, I held on to a couple of pages of notes. Just as you suspected. But I couldn't bear sharing her at the time. I was stupid. Now are you happy? Now will you help me?

I just want to know what she thinks she's doing to me. Oh, I don't know. You're always telling me you can change anything you put your mind to. Well, now is definitely the time to prove it. Go to her house if you need to. You can play the concerned shrink. Just convince her to drop the charges and – if you can – to get in touch with me. If you think about it, this situation is as bad for you and the business as it is for me. We need to take some action. I can't do anything from here without them threatening to lock me up again. So it's up to you, Aubrey.

I don't mean to teach you – your own methods always seem surprisingly effective – but if I were you I would go with the sympathetic line. I tried confronting her in my letter and she reported me to the police. Don't underestimate her. You'll be tempted to do that when you see her house. It's all Arts and Crafts: mismatched second-hand furniture and hand-painted details on the shelves and skirting boards. Can you believe I ever thought that kind of nonsense was charming? It all just seemed so comfortable and feminine. I think there might be a housemate, but I never met her. Maybe she's responsible for the touches around the house, but I doubt it. The whole place reeks of Alice.

Oh, Aubrey, is there any hope for me? All I ever did was try to love her. Just as I loved Sarah.

Do your best for me.

Daniel

180

21st April
The Studio

Dear Mab –

Why haven't you written to me? Did I not manage to sound desperate enough in my last letter? Also, we are running low on funds. I tried to contact Claggy about the portrait sales, but I can't get past her assistant. Surely there must be some serious money coming our way? Or should I say your way? I suppose I'm out of the picture now I'm the accused.

Dad's not doing too well at the moment. I'm worried that we might have a recurrence of the urine infection. He's not acting crazy or anything, he just seems quiet and out of sorts. He and Tatty sleep all day. I don't have the energy to keep him up. The problem is, he's then up all night, knocking about in the dark. I've made sure the doors are all locked and bolted before I go to bed. I keep the keys in my room. There's no chance of him getting out into the street. Still, it's quite unnerving coming downstairs in the morning. He's usually broken something or hurt himself. And then he goes to sleep in the most unlikely places. I found him curled up in a pile of washing this morning with Tatty tucked in at his belly.

I guess I haven't been the best son lately. My own problems have been so overwhelming I don't seem to have anything left over to give him. There has been no word from Maggie or Sarah, despite their promises to call. We are so isolated here. So completely alone. I could do with some help. And the whisky supply is running low.

Daniel

30th April
The Studio

Dear Dad –

You'll probably never read this letter. You're in hospital. They've warned me you're not likely to return. It seems I've let you down. It's strange here. Maggie took Tatty away, so it's just me and the walls.

Mab wrote to me at last. She might be there with you on the ward now. She told me not to write to Freya any more. I've only sent silly little letters to her from Tatty. Well, you know all about them; you watched me write them. I knew she would love that dog. I am not to contact Mab either. The women have closed me off and left me behind.

I can't return to Manchester. It doesn't seem right while you're still here. Alive, if not kicking. That's more or less what the nurse told me over the phone. I pretended to be your nephew; I wasn't sure whether they'd let me know anything if I gave my real name. I am too disgraceful to deserve any information.

There is too much light. I've drawn the curtains, but it creeps through and squats on the rug. Impossible to ignore. It's this damn spring, bringing more hours of daylight every day. I am much happier in a gloom, both figurative and literal. I wait until dark before leaving the house. Thank goodness for the late-night shop under the bridge. And the bored exchange of girls behind the counter. That's where I get the papers. I suppose I should ignore them – it was inevitable that someone would pick up the story – but I don't see why they had to drag your name into it. None of them is above the intrusion. There's this from the local rag:

Not a Pretty Picture:
Laird Family Rape Allegations

The son of famous artist Michael Laird was arrested earlier this month following his father's triumphant comeback exhibition.

Charges of rape and harassment were levelled at Daniel Laird following complaints from an unnamed source. Sources suggest that these alleged crimes took place in Greater Manchester, in which area he had previously resided. Thanks to publicity for his father's PORTRAITS showcase, police were able to track Laird and conduct the arrest.

Laird, since released on bail, was born and schooled in Upchurch. He was described by Mr J. Hunting of Upchurch High School as a 'large, awkward boy' who 'kept himself to himself'. Not much is known of his movements since his return to the area, though rumours suggest that several other women have come forward since Laird's arrest was made public.

The Laird family are keen to distance themselves from possible scandal. Michael Laird was too unwell to comment, but Mabel Laird (the artist's daughter from his first marriage) pleaded for 'privacy at this difficult time'.

Nice to hear that things are difficult for Mab. No real mention of what it's like to play the monster of the piece. Well, it's not much fun, let me tell you. And the picture they included is far from flattering. I suppose they could have used one of your portraits of me. One should be grateful for small mercies.

I'm drinking too much. I'm finishing off what's left of the whisky. And I don't have your excuse. I'm perfectly aware of my actions. I know how tragic my situation is. In fact, I'm even guilty of enjoying it. I can see it as the opening scene of a movie: the camera panning from the drawn curtains to the man in his chair. A glass by his side, smeared with greasy fingerprints. The man is unshaven and his clothing creased. When he's not writing on the pad of paper in front of him, he stares forward and his lips move. The changes of expression suggest he's rehearsing some conversation. Some argument he cannot win. I've dabbled with the idea of a soundtrack, maybe something classical and baroque, but I don't think it's necessary. The set-up is clichéd enough without music. Let the viewer struggle to make out what the man is saying and what he is writing. Let them be content with the small shuffle of pen and cuff against paper.

Not much of a beginning, but I must be content with the cards I have been dealt. I have to make the best of things, isn't that what Maggie would say? Do you know what she left me, as a house-leaving gift, when she came to get Tatty. A cyclamen. It's sitting next to me now. Dark red blooms with sharp waxy leaves, balanced on an open hand of rounded stems. I considered using it as an ashtray, but I couldn't bring myself to stub out my cigarette in the soil. It will die soon, I'm sure – there's not enough light in here – but for the moment it is healthy and fresh. I've even watered it a couple of times on my way back from the bathroom. An unlikely pool of life in this dour room, and my only companion.

Maybe a plant is a safer pet for me than Tatty, but I miss the excuse to take a walk. There is nothing more anonymous than a man with a dog. I miss you too, of course, but Maggie was right. I wasn't taking care of either of you in the right way. I must learn to accept my punishment. It may not be long until they put me back in a prison cell. I suppose I should get used to solitary.

The new complaints to the police. They haven't told me, but it has become pretty clear where they're coming from. Another gift from Maggie was to give me Sarah's name. The betrayal was overwhelming. To claim that our night together all those years ago was anything but the fulfilment of both our desires. And to think she carried such hatred and bitterness towards me. I am so stupid. When I first came back here, it was you I was afraid of, but, all the while, lies were breeding in the minds of those I thought to love. Despite all my research and work, I played the game wrong. Another punishment to shoulder.

Mab was very strange in her letter. There was more written there than the simple order against contact. She managed to destroy not only our future relationship, but our history as well. I don't understand any of it. She said that she was forced to go into league with Aubrey to get rid of me when I turned up in Corsica. She even claimed to have paid him to keep me 'safe' – whatever that means. Now he's proved himself unable to complete that one task, their understanding is at an end. According to Mab, I don't have a job to go back to. And I don't have her to run to. I have nowhere else to be. Nowhere else where I am welcome. This room is my only refuge. So I must sit in it alone and learn to be grateful.

(Later)

I walked to the shop under the bridge. The girl behind the counter smiled at me and said hello as I walked in. Obviously not a big reader. I just went in to pick up a couple of TV dinners; I had to ask for the bottle of whisky.

'Big night?'

'I'm sorry?'

'It was a joke. A bad joke.'

They were the first words I'd spoken aloud for five days. *I'm sorry*. And I'd chosen to share them with the girl with the bad haircut and bitten nails who was scanning my macaroni cheese. Maybe I should settle down with her, I thought. Maybe if I could just make her smile again, then we could start to chat and she could tell me about her family and her troubles. We could hold hands over the counter. Exchange chaste kisses while people browsed for their breakfast cereal and emergency pints of milk, separating only when they came to the till. They'd smile on us – the passing custom – and think us oh so sweet. I'd bring her presents. Maybe some kind of capsicum pepper solution to paint her nails with. Thoughtful things, wrapped up in bright paper.

'I just love to watch your face when you open them,' I'd say.

'You shouldn't spoil me.'

But I would spoil her. I'd bring her chocolates and home-made peppermint creams – to keep her blood sugar up on the long night-shift. On our weekly anniversary, I'd play at being the customer and she'd tell her joke and I'd laugh and give her red roses, one for every day I'd known her. It would be beautiful.

This was what I was thinking as I walked home in the dark. I was forgetting to keep to my urban fox route, in the shadows. And that was when I met Maggie. She tried to ignore me at first, I think. But I called out to her and asked her how you were doing.

'He broke his hip. He's still in the hospital, what do you think? And where you should be, if anybody thought to ask me, is by his bedside like a proper son. You need to start acting right, Danny. You should be ashamed of yourself.'

'Mab won't let me be there.'

'And when have you ever listened to that sister of yours? And whose fault is it that the poor man is in that bed in the first place? When I think of what you put him through, with me round the corner and just a phone call away. Sweet Jesus, I'm so angry I can't even look at you.

'And here you are. Look at the state of you. You look and smell like you've slept in those clothes. And you are not one of those men who can wear a beard. I've told you. Is that what you've been doing back there, wallowing in self-pity? Well, I tell you, there are more people out there deserving of your pity and some of them not so far away.'

They say:

I didn't take care of you.
It was my fault you fell.
Without Tatty's bark and howl, they would never have known you lay on the bathroom floor. The neighbour would never have found you with your face pressed against the break in the lino, your breath shallow and faint. You were still trying to pull the pair of clean dress trousers over the

split catheter bag, over your shattered hip. I don't know where you could have found them.

They found empty bottles around the bottom of my chair and no food in the fridge.

No one could wake me – not even the ambulance men – to tell me what had happened to you. When they tried, I got abusive. They left me a note and let me sleep it off.

There were marks on your body. Cuts, abrasions, bruises and sores. There was a dark, angry rash on your lower leg where the urine had soaked into your skin.

They had to cut Tatty's fur to get the filth out. Special solvent and special food had to be bought to get her back to her normal self.

I should be prosecuted.

I should be in prison.

You wouldn't treat a dog that way.

I shouldn't have treated a dog that way.

I say:

I seem to have lost myself somewhere in everyone else's opinion.

I have only ever tried to do my best. To be the best man I could be. The best son, the best brother, the best lover, the best friend. I have never managed to be the best at anything.

I misjudged you. You were the one I should have turned to. You were the only one who could have understood me.

I lose everything that I love.

I'm writing this letter to you, but you'll never read it. I've run out of readers.

I'm sure they'll arrest me in the morning and I only owe one person an apology. I have only done one thing wrong.

I'm sorry, Dad.

Acknowledgements

With thanks to all those who read and encouraged me through early drafts, in particular David Hill, Elspeth Latimer, Hayley Webster, Tom Corbett, Sarah Butler and Alice Kuipers. Thanks are due to Writers' Centre Norwich for their support and care. Also, to the Literary Consultancy and their Free Read scheme. And Syd Moore, Colette Bailey and all at METAL Southend, who gave me fresh perspective and helped me find the right ending.

This novel found publication through the Myriad Writer's Retreat Competition. I must thank Candida Lacey and Pam McIlroy (*aka* Pamreader) for belief in the book and their continued kindness to its author. To all at Myriad Editions for their tireless work and support, but, most of all, thanks to Holly Ainley, editor and friend, for reading it and reading it and always believing in it.

Finally, thank you to my family: to Mum, Heidi and John, to whom this book is dedicated, for saving me and loving me and reading pages even when you really didn't want to. And to David, Mary and Alice, the loves of my life, for showing me a happiness I didn't know existed when I started this book.

MORE FROM MYRIAD

MORE FROM MYRIAD

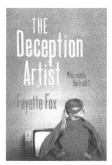

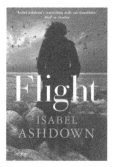

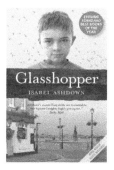

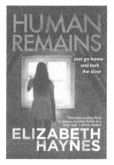

MORE FROM MYRIAD

MORE FROM MYRIAD

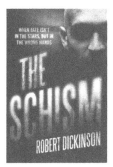

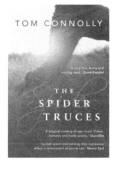

Sign up to our mailing list at
www.myriadeditions.com
Follow us on Facebook and Twitter

S.E. Craythorne lives and works in rural
Norfolk. She holds an MA in Creative
Writing from the University of East Anglia
and her poetry and prose have been
published in various literary journals.
How You See Me is her first novel.